Over The Edge

N.D. Lewis

Over the Edge
2017© by N. D. Lewis
ISBN-13: 978-1542661874

All rights reserved. No part of this publication may be reproduced, distributed, or transmitted in any form or by any means, including photocopying, recording, or other electronic or mechanical methods, without the prior written permission of the publisher, except in the case of brief quotations embodied in critical reviews and certain other noncommercial uses permitted by copyright law.

For permission requests, write to the publisher, addressed "Attention: Permissions Coordinator," at the email address below.

info@ndlewis.com
www.ndlewis.com

Dedication

To pain.

How would I have ever known what a remarkable human I could be without you.

Chapter 1

Ivy sat in the waiting room of the doctor's office patiently waiting for them to call her name. Although she wasn't afraid of this particular visit, it wasn't one she had been looking forward to. The truth is, after any trauma people are nervous about hearing what the doctor's report may be especially when you can't really divulge the entire truth about why you're in the condition that you're in. Finally, Ivy wouldn't have to worry about that. She would be free to talk to this doctor in detail about everything she had just experienced and its effect on her life since.

"Ms. Kasey?" the receptionist called. As she spotted Ivy amid the small group of people waiting, she motioned for her to come into the doctor's office.

Ivy was always a big fan of free flowing long dresses that complimented her full figure and now with almost seven months of new life protruding from her stomach, her wardrobe was more of a comfort then she'd ever imagined. Her chubby brown face was glowing with hormones in a navy blue dress that swept over her white polished toenails, matching the crisp, white knit blazer. She slowly wobbled her way into the office and the gold bangles on her wrist clanged together as she reached across the table and shook hands with the doctor before sitting down.

"It's good to finally meet you Ms. Kasey."

"You too Dr. Gilbert."

"Please have a seat here and make yourself as comfortable as you can." Dr. Gilbert helped Ivy to a very comfortable sofa and placed a firm pillow behind her back.

Dr. Julia Gilbert was a short, stubby, light-skinned African-American woman somewhere around her mid 50's. Outfitted in a very conservative dark brown pants suit. Her coarse grey hair was cut in short bob, with a few remaining streaks of her natural brunette hair color peeking through. Ivy was glad to be sitting down with her as she came so highly recommended.

"Thank you so much," Ivy replied to her kindness.

"You're most welcome. You have a full package there I want to make sure you're comfortable," Dr. Gilbert laughed.

"I appreciate it."

"You're at about seven months now right?"

"That's right!" she said rubbing her tummy.

"Is it a boy or girl?"

"I don't know yet. We wanted it to be a surprise so we're waiting. Although, I'm getting extremely anxious."

"I just bet you are! Well, before we get started I want to remind you that I am licensed and hired through the federal government specifically for grief and trauma therapy for cases such as yours. As you requested, I am a Christian therapist and with your permission I have reviewed your file. I am aware of what you have experienced in detail and you will not have any restraints on what you can discuss with me. Just like any other case, you have the benefit of Doctor/Patient confidentiality."

"That's good to know," Ivy exhaled in relief.

"Now you understand that I'll be seeing both, you and Jack, separately. Then, after we've completed those sessions we'll bring the two of you together."

"Okay. How long will we be separate?"

"Well, that depends on the two of you and when you feel like you're ready. You aren't currently living together are you?"

"No," Ivy answered quickly.

"Okay, that's good right now believe it or not. When was the last time you saw each other?"

"Well, we see each other just about every day. I take care of his..." Ivy paused, "Well, now, our daughter Melanie, when he's at work except when she's with her grandmother."

"Well, why we don't begin by you telling me why you're here."

Ivy's first thought was, "Is that was a trick question?" If she's read the file, then clearly Dr. Gilbert knew why she was sitting there. Jack and Ivy had spent the last five months trying to piece their lives back together and they hadn't been very successful. It wasn't because they didn't try to love each other back to the middle, but it had proven to be much harder than they both were prepared for. Their last hope of making it work was agreeing to separate and commit to this therapy.

"Not to be rude, but I thought it was obvious why I was here, Dr. Gilbert."

"Please, call me Julia."

"Okay, Julia, I'm not sure I understand what you mean."

"Let me share something with you. Look at my arm," Julia lifted her arm so that Ivy could see the dark brown scar that stretched from her wrist to above her elbow. "You see this scar here? This scar makes it obvious that something happened to me. You can tell that whatever happened there was deep, it was painful and happened a long time ago. What you can't see is how and why it happened, if there has been any healing beneath the surface or how, or if, I still suffer from it. So again, why don't you tell me why you are here?"

Ivy shook her head as she realized the depth of the question before her. True, it was obvious that trauma had brought her here, but she herself didn't even know how deep that trauma was and that's why she was here. She looked up at the ceiling and sighed.

"I'm here because… I feel like I'm unraveling and I don't know how to stop it."

"What's the biggest thing you feel is coming apart?"

"My relationship with Jack. I feel like we may have started coming apart before Cuba and then after it we tried to just be together as if our issues weren't our issues just because they seemed so petty in comparison to the accident."

"Incident," Julia said matter-of-factly.

"Excuse me?"

"It was not an accident, Ivy. Someone intentionally and methodically tried to rob you of your life. The only accident was for Lisa because you survived and she didn't. To say you had 'an accident' gives your would-be killers a way out of owning what they did when, in fact, complete responsibility belongs to them."

Ivy immediately felt anger and frustration.

"But, they can't accept responsibility can they? To do that would mean to have to come face to face with those you tried to hurt and either accept your punishment or beg for forgiveness and they can't do either!"

"So you think their deaths were merciful?"

"I think death was easy. It showed them kindness and offers me nothing. So to insinuate that someone can take responsibility now is pointless," said a very cold Ivy.

"It is only pointless if you believe that your life isn't worth more than the weight of carrying a burden that no one living is able to bear. Ivy, you had a life before Cuba and seeing as how God spared it, you obviously have one to live after it. Trauma doesn't afford us the luxury of living ignorantly in duality. It forces us to choose to live consciously in either, what was, or what is. You have to decide where you want to live."

Ivy was blotting her eyes that were now melting with the tears she had fought to hold back. It was only the first hour in the first day of therapy and she was already sobbing. She realized the importance of the decision that sat before her. The challenge was that, other than the terror that she endured in Cuba, she loved everything about her life before that happened. Years of self-discovery had gone into becoming the woman she was and it had proven successful in many ways and to decide to let it all go and start over in the space she was in now was frightening. Ivy, however, was courageous if she was anything at all. If anything in her life was worth fighting for, it was Jack.

"I want to live in what is," Ivy confessed.

"Good. Now, let's work on getting you there."

They both took a few deep breaths and Dr. Gilbert continued with pad and pencil in hand. "Five months ago, after a few weeks in the hospital, you were released to go home. Let's begin there."

Chapter 2

It was a cool, Sunday morning in October when Ivy was finally being released from the hospital. It had been three weeks since her fiancé, Detective Jack Benett found her near death on a small stretch of beach in Cuba. A terrible incident had left her with numerous stitches in the head and some badly bruised ribs. Due to, not only the physical, but emotional trauma she had endured, the staff at McLaren Regional Hospital in her hometown of Flint, Michigan had kept a very close eye on her…and her unborn child.

Now, after a lot of consideration, her long time physician Dr. Julius Simon, was ready to send her home. Ivy, who was used to working, was not at all thrilled to be forced to sit still for so long and was more than ready to get back home. Jack, of course, wanted them to take every precaution with his wife-to-be so he didn't mind waiting until she checked out clear.

The first week in the hospital, Ivy spent in and out of consciousness, undergoing multiple tests to make sure that all the water in her lungs had been drained properly and that she had suffered no further internal injuries. Although she was very glad they were taking exceptional care, Ivy was very sick of being poked and prodded. Every day it was something else to test or check all the while she was undergoing various interviews for police records so they could complete all the paperwork about the case that caused her injuries. Even though they were sending her home, Ivy had a very long recovery ahead of her. Jack was going to see to it that she did indeed recover and got back to her normal self, or as close as possible.

"Dr. Simon, will you kindly remind my fiancé that, although she is going home, she still has to take it easy," Jack said as he knew Ivy would try to get right back to work.

"Oh, yes, Ms. Ivy, you still have a ways to go to be fully prepared to get back into work. You must give your body time to recover. You are only ten weeks into your pregnancy and, with your history of adrenal fatigue and chronic hypoglycemia, it's imperative that you avoid stress at all costs." Dr. Simon was adamant about his patient relaxing and getting the rest she needed. He knew her and her medical history very well. Stress and Ivy Kasey did not mix well at all.

"Don't worry doctor, I have no intention of over-doing it. I will be working from home for quite a while," confessed the still very frail Ivy.

"Good. I want you to be careful still, I know how involved you get with your work. Just take it easy. Let's get you to at least sixteen weeks before you get moving anywhere close to normal okay?"

"Yes, Dr. Simon."

"Thank you, Doc," Jack said shaking his hand. "I will call if she needs a reminder."

"Okay you do that."

Ivy's mother began to collect her things and get her signed out. Once all of the paperwork was done and she was cleared to leave, Jack went ahead to get the car and her mother wheeled her toward the exit.

She hated to be seated in that wheelchair, but it was hospital policy. Ivy was stubborn and was not very accepting of displays of weakness, however now was not the time to try and pretend that she was okay. She had been through a great deal of trauma and now her main priority was bringing a healthy baby into the world. That would override her desire to get back on the road. Ivy was content to stay at home to rest and to write. Besides, after that whole scene in Cuba she had new bestseller in her mind that had to get onto paper.

It was a quick, but a seemingly long ride as she sat there in the wheelchair still very grateful that she was alive. Ivy wasn't sure if it was her hormones or if she was just overwhelmed with gratitude, but she had been crying every day since she opened her eyes in that hospital and realized she was back home. It was still very surreal to her that just three weeks ago Jack had rescued her after his ex-girlfriend Lisa, the mother of his first born, had literally tried to kill her.

Jack had no idea who this woman really was when he got involved with her. Lisa Durant, a.k.a. Isabel Dumayas, had taken charge of the Cuban Mafia after her grandfather's passing and was the puppeteer behind his nephew being kidnapped three years ago. When Jack didn't respond to Lisa the way she wanted, she went after Ivy and almost succeeded.

Ivy didn't remember much of what actually happened that night in Cuba due the head injury. After she had opened that hotel room door, Lisa and her brother Sammie had pushed through the door, knocking Ivy backward onto a glass table. Lisa then, kicked Ivy several times and then Sammie dragged the unconscious Ivy's near lifeless body out of the hotel room like a rag doll. Once they had finished their abuse, they left her for dead at the edge of the water.

Ivy didn't know at the time that she was pregnant. It was nothing short of a miracle that she didn't lose the baby. No matter how unreal it may have seemed, it all had really happened and Ivy had the unfortunate scars to prove it. God had really shown up for her and again it brought tears to her eyes as she approached the exit doors of the hospital.

She pulled some tissue out of her bag and blotted her eyes. Ivy laughed as she watched Jack struggle to clear out the truck so she could get in. His car was an absolute mess from the last few weeks. He barely went home because he was too busy clearing loads of paperwork at work and checking on Ivy daily. Not to mention that he was now a full-time father. His daughter, Mel, was in and out of the car and back and forth to his parent's house. Jack was a good man and Ivy was just incredibly satisfied with what God had given her. The happy tears kept falling. This man had risked everything to save her and for a girl who was afraid of being carried away with love, she was now very happily settled on cloud nine.

"He's the one, mommy. Jack is the one," Ivy declared aloud as she grabbed her mother's hand and pressed it up against her face.

"Of course, he is! I knew it all along, baby girl," Mother Kasey confessed smiling proudly. She had always liked Jack and he had definitely proven himself worthy to take care of her baby.

"Oh, you knew it all along? Why didn't you tell me?" she laughed.

"Some things you have find out for yourself baby. I'm sad it took all this craziness for you two to get it, but at least I get a grandbaby out of the deal."

"I hope you're not disappointed in me. I never wanted to embarrass you or the family."

"Oh, hush, girl. You're alive and you have life growing in you. I'm happy in Jesus!" Mother Ivette Chatman-Kasey was so old school and her baby girl, Ivy, adored her.

It felt good to know her mother was supportive of her and Jack. Although they were officially engaged now, they hadn't spent one minute in the last few weeks talking about a wedding. The main concern was Ivy getting well and getting home. Since her cousin Kayla was set to get married in two months, she got out of her lease early and decided to move in with Ivy until the wedding. Mother Kasey had another week off that she would spend in Rochester with Ivy as well. She no longer had federal agents protecting her day and night but Ivy had plenty of people looking after her.

As of last week Jack's case was publicly closed and the government had officially declared that there was no longer any threat to Jack or Ivy. Lisa and her brother were dead and with no official leader of an already small Cuban Mafia, the remaining parts were unraveling right into the hands of the FBI. Although it was a huge relief for the soon to be Mr. & Mrs. Jack Benett, it would never be life as usual. Too much had occurred and their lives were changed forever. It was a fairly quiet ride back home.

Chapter 3

"So you acknowledged before you left the hospital that day, that no matter what you did your life would never be the same?" Dr. Gilbert interjected.

"Yes I did… I knew things would be different. Just not this different," replied a solemn Ivy.

"I can understand. Please, continue."

"I remember riding quietly in the backseat of the truck on the way home. Everything looked so much different, but I knew nothing had changed except me."

Trauma has a way of altering one's perception. Things that used to go by unnoticed like a simple wind blowing through the trees, now seemed so beautiful and yet frightening. She was thrilled to have life, but suspicious of her surroundings. It was something she couldn't seem to let go. Ivy had ignored her instincts before and was determined never to do it again. She knew Lisa was bad news, but she kept quiet in order to keep the peace. From now on, she would always be aware, she would always be alert and no harm would come to her, or her family, as long as she had breath.

Uncomfortable with the silence in the car, Mother Kasey thought it best to use the time to discuss the upcoming nuptials of the newly engaged couple.

"So, have you two talked about a wedding date yet? Will we be waiting until after the baby is born?"

"We haven't talked it about it yet, mother," Jack said while Ivy remained quiet, "What do you think?" Jack asked his future mother-in-law.

"No, no, no this is your wedding now. You two must decide," Mother Kasey replied humbly.

"Well, I know wedding planning can get kind of stressful and I would rather not add something that big to our plate right now. I think the main thing is to make sure Ivy and the baby are getting enough rest. What do you think Lady?"

"I agree honey," Ivy said quietly. Her mother and Jack both knew Ivy was excited about getting married, but the wedding itself wasn't something she seemed happy about planning.

"Well, you have time. No rush. I think it's good for you both to take some time and rest."

Mother Kasey was relieved that they agreed not to put the extra pressure of wedding planning on themselves right now. Everything would happen all in good time, but now it was time to rest and regain their strength. Jack however didn't have the luxury of time. He was being subpoenaed to court in Washington D.C. to finish this business with the federal government and he had to leave in the morning. He was waiting until Ivy was home to tell her. By the time they pulled into her driveway he was still trying to figure out how to give her the news.

Kayla was at Ivy's house and had been in there for the last week moving in and setting up the house so Ivy could be comfortably settled downstairs. Doctor's orders were to keep her away from stairs and any extensive physical activity until she cleared sixteen weeks of pregnancy with zero complications. Physically, Ivy was weak and, even in the hospital, she had lost just over twenty pounds in only three weeks. They weren't too concerned because she had plenty of pounds to spare, but the baby needed to keep growing and they would let nothing interfere.

As they slowly walked into the house, Kayla met her cousin at the door with a big hug.

"Oh I'm so glad you're home!"

"It's good to be home," Ivy cried still in her embrace. Kayla grabbed her hand and walked her into the living room.

"Come on, you have to see this!"
They walked into the living room and it was full with many of Ivy's family members. Both of her sisters, her cousins, aunts, uncles, band members, including Curtis, and her precious god-son, Manny was there. Her brother hadn't made it up north just yet but had been checking on her daily while she was in the hospital. They didn't want to startle her so they all whispered, "Surprise!" with great, silly grins covering their faces. Ivy cried.

"What are you all doing here?" Ivy cried asked overwhelmed with emotion.

"This is your welcome home/engagement party!" Kayla declared. Mother Kasey had informed the family that Ivy had been in an accident. Due to the confidentiality of the case they were not allowed to tell the family all of the details, but they were a very close knit family so, once the news got out, they all rushed in to welcome her home.

Jack carefully walked Ivy to the new recliner he bought for her. Still rolling out light tears of joy, she had a seat as each family member one by one came over to hug her and congratulate her on her engagement. Each one was very cautious as they embraced her, not knowing Ivy was carrying something very special.

That whole scene in Cuba had strengthened all of their faith in God. Of course, at the same time, it brought along some added discomfort that they didn't have before. Ivy's family wasn't externally associated with drama. Granted, inside the family there was a lot of unnecessary chaos going on that they couldn't seem to get right, but it stayed inside. They weren't the kind of people you would hear about on the news having brawls and being a part of any kind of criminal madness. Cuba would go down in history as the most extensive drama that had ever happened in the family and most of them would never know it had happened at all.

When the Chatman family gathered, it was common to do three things – eat, laugh and pray. Before the prayer over the food began, there was one more thing Ivy wanted to add to the list of things to cover. Ivy knew it was a miracle that she was home and the family could have very well been gathering for her funeral, but thanks be to God they were here to celebrate life.

Jack got everyone's attention as he stood next to his beautiful lady. They had agreed to share their joy and, after all, she had survived. Ivy had plenty of courage to tell her very conservative family that she was having a baby.

"I am so glad to see all you here," Ivy began in a frail voice, "You know this really could have been a different kind of gathering….", before Ivy could finish, her mother and two of her aunts had already began speaking in tongues and going into a Sunday morning kind of praise. Ivy began to cry as she looked up at Jack and shook her head. He knew she was done talking. He would have to take over her speech.

"It means a lot to us that you all are here. There are many of you that I have yet to get to know but I thank you for being such a beautiful family. You have produced this wonderful lady that I am honored to soon call my wife." Jack stalled as he saw the family on pins and needles just waiting to hear what could possibly be next.

"It wasn't just Ivy's life God saved in that accident, we are grateful to announce that we're also having a baby!"

It was like a bomb went off as all the women in the room started screaming and cheering. They had been waiting for Ivy to have a baby. If she was born to do anything it was to be a mother. Although they didn't too much expect her to be pregnant before the marriage, everyone was still very happy for her.

So they prayed for the food, the continued growth and success of the family and for Ivy. It was now officially a Chatman family event, but it wouldn't last as long as they usually do. Ivy needed her rest so they all kept that in mind and made sure they didn't crowd her. After a few hours, almost everyone was gone, or on their way out. Jack had gone outside to walk some folks out and a quiet Curtis took the opportunity to speak to Ivy alone. He sat down on the cherry wood coffee table in front of her chair and grabbed her hand.

"So this is it, huh? You're getting married... and having his baby...?" Curtis questioned with clear discontent.

"Yes, this is it, Curtis," Ivy replied.

"So, how you feelin'?"

"Honestly... I'm really glad to be home... but I'm so tired and still really sore."

"I should think so. You did get your ribs kicked in due to..."

"Don't Curtis," she interrupted. She wasn't going to let him pull her into that conversation. "Jack saved us. You understand? If it was not for him I wouldn't be here. He is my choice." Just as she was stating that, Jack had walked back into the house.

"Who is Curtis?" Dr. Gilbert asked interrupting Ivy's recollection of the past.

"Curtis Howard was my Manager/Producer and member of the band I sang with at the time. We had been friends for about five years before I met Jack."

"Was he a threat to your relationship?"

"In some ways," Ivy admitted. "Curtis knew my heart belonged to Jack, but that wasn't something he was willing to accept at that time. In the past, every time Jack wasn't there, which always seemed to be at bad time for me, Curtis was there. And I let him be there rather than be alone," Ivy said acknowledging that she had contributed to Curtis being a problem, but also that she had tried to correct it.

"I was making things clear to him the day I came home after that party. When Jack walked back into the house and saw us talking, he didn't say anything, but I could feel him glaring at us. He never did like Curtis."

"Did you like Curtis? In an intimate way?" Dr. Gilbert questioned.

"I did. Curtis was my friend and I loved him. Now we had never slept together but we were very intimate in a non-sexual way if that's makes sense."

"Yes, I understand, but why did you need that when you had Jack?"

"Because I didn't always have Jack."

"You're referring to before you two met?"

"No. Before and after we met."

"Can you explain?"

"While in our relationship, Jack was not always there when I needed him primarily because of his job. When he didn't show up for me, Curtis would, and I embraced that. But I wasn't consciously trying to give him that space that belonged to Jack."

"So, what were you trying to do?"

Ivy pursed her lips tight and sighed.

"I was trying to prevent from having to say out loud that I wasn't getting everything I needed in my relationship. I never talked bad about Jack to Curtis, but he knew when things were off simply by the joy I had with his presence at the times that Jack had not shown up for me."

"Why not just talk to Jack and ask for what you needed?"

"It should be so simple," Ivy laughed. "But, I feared that if I told Jack what I needed…all he would hear was me insulting him because, in his mind, there is nothing he wouldn't do for me. Then, I'd be the reason he felt bad. He'd shut down and we would get nowhere."

"So, when you told Curtis that Jack is your choice that day, how did he respond to Jack?"

"Curtis looked up and saw Jack walking towards us and he stood up, held out his hand and Jack received it and they shook hands in this very awkward silence." Ivy recalled, as she returned to the story.

"Congratulations," Curtis said unexpectedly.

"Thank you," Jack replied, suspiciously.

"I'm heading out, but, um…I wanted to say thank you. I appreciate you bringing her home."

"It was my pleasure," Jack was surprised by Curtis' words but very glad he seemed accepting of the new status of his relationship. Even still, Ivy was sure Jack would have his final words with Curtis, but not in front of her. Curtis hugged Ivy then, he and Jack walked out to the car.

"Did you ask Jack what he said to Curtis outside?" Dr. Gilbert interrupted again.

"I did, but not that day. I had planned to, but I got side-tracked."

"What happened?"

"Pain. The medicine was starting to wear off and so I needed to quickly get in the shower and take the next dose if I was going to get any sleep."

"So when did this conversation come up again between you and Jack?"

"Months later."

"Hmm... Continue."

"Okay, so I knew it was time to say goodnight. The medication they had me on was so strong that within a half hour of taking it I would be in a very deep sleep."

Ivy explained how she had slowly eased her way out of her new favorite chair in the house and tried to quietly make her way to bathroom to get ready for bed. Now that everyone was making their way out of the house, Kayla and Mother Kasey were in the kitchen cleaning up. They were in the midst of discussing the hilarious family nuances when they heard what sounded like glass breaking in the other room.

"Ivy?" Kayla yelled form the kitchen.

When she didn't get a response, they ran looking for her and found her outside the bathroom door bowed over against the wall. She had accidently knocked over a vase while trying to grab her bag from the floor. Bending over was proving to be very difficult and not something she should have been trying to do.

"What are you in here doing child?" her mother shouted.

"Mom, I'm fine I was just trying to get my medicine," Ivy said trying to make sure they didn't overreact. But it was already too late for that.

"The doctor said you shouldn't be bending over like this. Just ask for some help, girl!" Kayla barked at her. True to form, Ivy was hard-headed and trying too soon to be independent. Her mother grabbed her bag and walked with her into the bathroom.

"Maybe you should shower, then take your medicine. This stuff is strong the last thing you need to do is to fall in the tub," Mother Kasey said.

Mother Kasey turned on the shower and helped her baby girl undress. It wasn't until this moment that Ivy realized how much help she really needed. Although she felt really good inside, on the outside her body was still suffering. Ivy was very glad to have her mommy with her.

Chapter 4

Jack wasn't convinced that therapy was the solution, but he was convinced that he couldn't continue to live this way. He was uncomfortable with every moment Ivy lived in question about his love for her. So, if it was going to take committing to this uncomfortable intrusion to make her believe, then this is what he would do.

In his head he had said it was only for her, but in his heart Jack knew he was way past due for therapy. Too many things had taken place between his career, family and love life that were mentally, and emotionally, exhausting. Without his permission, these things were invading every facet his life. Now the price of therapy had become much more affordable than the price of ignorance and avoidance.

"Mr. Benett?" the receptionist called. "Dr. Gilbert will see you now. Please follow me."

Jack stood tall on his strong legs in his dark stressed blue jeans and broad shoulders gently concealed inside in the high collar burgundy cable-knit sweater. The moment he walked into a room he was, without trying, an intimidating force of masculinity. He was a big chocolate bear of a man, but surprisingly gentle in almost every step he took.

Jack politely shook hands with Dr. Gilbert before he sat down in a chair. He wouldn't dare sit on that couch or get too comfortable. Although he had agreed to come, he still had the steel walls of defense up. Every officer was subject to mandatory sessions at least once a year so he knew the basics of what was about to happen, but this time it was much more personal.

"Mr. Benett, since we're both officers I will spare you my opening speech because you're well aware of the drill. I will, however, remind you that the agreement was for us to complete our individual sessions before you and Ms. Kasey come together. Is that alright?" Dr. Gilbert asked.

"How long will that be?" Jack asked.

Dr. Gilbert grinned inside. They both had asked the same question, which told her that neither of them really wanted to be apart.

"That depends on the two of you and when you think you're ready, but by my assumption it'll only be about three weeks."

"Okay."

"So, why are you here Mr. Benett?"

"I told Ivy I would come."

"Did you want to come?"

"No."

"So is your presence here just to appease her?"

"I'll do whatever it takes to make her happy."

"Are you happy?"

"Not now."

"Why?"

Jack sighed.

"Because for whatever reason I'm not making her happy."

"Were you happy the day you brought her home from the hospital?"

"Oh yeah," Jack smiled as his thoughts quickly went back to that day. "... I was very happy."

"Okay. Take me back to that day."

"Well... I remember her mother pushing her out of the front doors of the hospital in this old blue wheelchair and she was smiling." He grinned as he remembered thinking of how incredible Ivy was. Even in that moment she looked like she was filled with optimism. "She was smiling like… like nothing had ever happened to her," he said, shaking his head. "I got her home and her cousin had secretly planned a gathering of her family so they would know she was okay. I was a little concerned about just how much they knew. So I pulled Kayla aside to find out."

"Hey Jack," Kayla said, "Sorry we didn't tell you, but we wanted this little party to be a surprise. What do you think?" she asked with excitement.

"I think this is really nice, but how much about what happened does your family know?" Jack whispered.

"They only know that Ivy had been in a really bad accident when we went to Cuba. They don't know anything about Lisa or the baby. I figured you guys would tell them if you wanted them to know. Is that okay?"

"Yeah, that's cool. Thanks."

"So what else is wrong?" Kayla knew there was more due to the look of worry on Jack's face.

"I've been subpoenaed to D.C. to finish this case. I only have to go for a couple days. I was hoping to tell Ivy about it, but not in front of all your family."

"Oh, okay, well when do you have to leave?"

He sighed, "Tomorrow morning…"

"No worries, Jack, just wait until after the party is over. Besides, her mother and I will be here so we'll take care of her."

"I don't want to leave her," he confessed. He was afraid now to be away from her.

"Jack, God didn't bring her though all this to let anything happened to her now. She'll be okay; I'll make sure of it," Kayla assured him.

It wasn't a long party, which was good for Ivy. Jack didn't want her to be overwhelmed so he was glad to be walking family members out to their cars after only a couple hours. He wasn't, however, glad to come back inside the house to see Curtis holding Ivy's hand. It didn't matter what he was saying to her, Jack just didn't like it and he walked over there to make sure Curtis knew it was time for him to go also.

"I was surprised when he stood up and shook my hand and even thanked me for bringing Ivy home." Jack stated as he remembered that day.

"What were you expecting from him?" Julia asked.

"I don't know. I just didn't trust him and he proved I had good reason. He played this role in front of Ivy, but when we got outside he had other things to say."

"Why didn't you trust him?"

"I know he'd known Ivy longer than I had and I know Curtis always wanted more out of their relationship. He always had that open window before I came along and he never accepted that the window was shut."

"What exactly was Curtis doing?"

"I just felt like whenever my back was turned he was there. Like if Ivy was doing something and I couldn't make it I knew he would always be there and I didn't like it. I felt like he should have respected our space. Then, again, if Ivy had respected it more maybe he would have, too"

"What do you mean?"

"I mean, when I wasn't there Ivy liked the fact that he was. If she didn't like it he would've stopped coming around. I just feel like he was a snake. A snake that was always trying to sneak his way in, but I also feel like she left the door open when I wasn't around."

"Was it often that you weren't around?"

"It wasn't like it was on purpose," Jack stated defensively. "It was almost always work related. There was nothing I could do. You know this job."

"Yes, I do. I also have learned that our job is one where very clear and tight boundaries need to be set. When we don't set them we begin to hide behind the work and we both know the damage it can do."

Julia had no need to play it easy with Jack. They both knew that there were choices they could make every day to make life a lot easier for their families who would sacrifice so much so the rest of the world could live in safety. Jack was fully aware, whether he wanted to admit it or not, that he hadn't set those boundaries. Unfortunately for him, Ivy wasn't ignorant to the rules of engagement. She knew some of those days he wasn't there for her was because he simply chose not to be.

"So, once you and Curtis get outside, what happens?"

Jack decided that he would once and for all make it very clear to Curtis that Ivy was completely off limits. He had no intention of upsetting her. So, he decided it was best to save his words as he walked Curtis out to his car. Outside in the driveway Curtis and Jack were having a very different conversation than the one they had in front of Ivy. Both men were committed to being nice and cordial for Ivy's sake. Now she was indoors and they were outdoors. All bets were officially off.

There was plenty of understandable tension between the two men and, now that they were finally alone, they were going to act on it. Physically they were no match whatsoever, so if they ever came to blows it would only take one hit from Jack for the disagreement to be settled, but it wouldn't come to that. Curtis' big smart mouth didn't match his small frame and when it came to Ivy he had no problem letting Jack know how he really felt.

"Look, dude, I know what you wanna say to me, but until I'm sure that nothing like what happened in Cuba will ever happen to her again, I will be watching very closely, whether you like it or not my brotha!" Curtis declared with the disrespectful intent.

"I couldn't care less how much you watch, but if I see you with your hands on my wife one more time we will have a problem... my brotha!"

"She's not your wife just yet. Bedsides, I'm really not the brother you should concerned about." Curtis hinted with a sly smirk.

"What's that supposed to mean?"

"You worried?" Curtis laughed.

"Not at all," Jack said, quickly and confidently.

"Maybe you should be, Detective!" Curtis insisted. "Ivy is one of kind and you should know you're not the only man that knows that," he said as got into his car.

In his mind, Jack could see himself punching Curtis right between the eyes and breaking every bone in his face. Instead, Jack just settled for being able to watch Curtis drive off knowing that he was the only man going inside to be with Ivy. It bothered him that Curtis suggested there was yet someone else who might hold Ivy's affections, but he decided to dismiss it. He had no space in his thoughts for those kinds of ideas. He brushed it off and went back inside the house.

"Did you really brush it off?" Julia asked interrupting the story. Curtis had inserted a very disturbing assumption into Jack's thoughts and she wanted to know how deep it actually got.

"I did at that time. I just felt like Curtis was grasping at straws to make me nervous because he never wanted Ivy and me to be together."

"Why do you think that was? He had known her much longer than you had so why do you think he was so against her being with you if it made her happy?"

"I think he was just jealous that I could do what he couldn't," Jack said arrogantly.

"Which was?"

"I made her happy. When she met me she didn't need him the same way anymore and he couldn't take it."

Jacks eyes suspiciously watched Dr. Gilbert's pen as she wrote swiftly the words he had just spoken. What Jack said was significant even though he wasn't clear what he meant by his own words, but apparently it struck a chord with the good doctor.

"So everyone has gone home now and the party was over, what happens next?" Dr. Gilbert inquired.

"I went inside the house and Kayla was finishing the rest of the dishes. She quickly asked me about what had happened with Curtis."

"So you and Curtis finally have it out?" Kayla asked, not shy about being nosy.

"Apparently not," Jack laughed "Don't look like your boy is giving up until the wedding day."

"Don't mind Curtis. He's a sore loser, but he's harmless. You can't blame him for being concerned can you?"

"I guess not. Where's my Lady?"

"She's taking a shower. She's taking her medicine right after so you might want to talk to her before that stuff kicks in."

"Right... Okay. Thanks, again, Kayla for doing all this."

"No problem."

Jack knocked on the bathroom door to let her know he was coming in. She was just turning off the water and asked him to hand her the towel that was sitting on top of the sink. Slowly, Ivy pulled back the blue dolphin covered curtain and even though she was smiling at him, Jack had tears welling up in his eyes.

He hadn't seen her naked body since before the accident and her once very smooth warm toffee skin was now a canvas of patch-worked bruises. She was only ten weeks pregnant and so to Jack, who knew every inch of her body better than his own, her weight loss was very noticeable. The burnt red bruises he had seen before around her neck and shoulders had darkened and were now big patches of purple and blue stretching from the top of her collarbone down to her legs. Every inch of her was only a reflection of the terror she had endured for the sake of their love.

"What did you feel when you looked at her?" Dr. Gilbert asked.

Jack was quiet. He wasn't sure if he could verbalize what he had felt in that moment.

"I was hurt …and I was angry, but …I felt… love. I loved her even more when I saw what she had gone through…just because she loved me. I was humbled," he said shaking his head. "I guess she could feel my mixed emotions and she held out her arms out for me." Jack smiled.

He walked toward her and wrapped her up in the towel and carefully placed his strong arms around her. As he helped her out of the shower he was cautious not to too hold her too tight. His little lady, who used to be quite sturdy and able to bear his strength, was now a very delicate flower and he didn't want to cause her any more pain. He held her gently inside of that towel and she rested her head on his warm chest. As the water bubbles on her hair began to melt into his shirt, Jack leaned his head down and kissed her forehead.

"I'm going to be okay Jack," she assured him. "Bruises hurt, but they heal Babe," she said as she looked up into those brown eyes that seized every strand of her love. "You're here and you make me whole," Ivy whispered to her love.

Jack couldn't figure it out and he had stopped trying, but there was something about this woman that just set his soul on fire. When it wasn't her words, it was her eyes, if not her eyes, then it was her voice, but she definitely held the key to his heart. Jack leaned down further and kissed her ever so softly on the lips.

Usually, he would intensify his embrace which, almost always, led to her back up against a wall, or door, or a mirror that would fall and crash on the floor, but he held back. One of the reasons he loved Ivy's plus-sized figure was because he knew she was capable of responding to his "hulkish" nature. He could grab her, swing her, or flip her and trust that she wouldn't break. Even though she was still his plus-sized chocolate rose, she was far too weak to be man-handled.

This was a new level of trust for them both. It's easy to love when everything you see is pleasing to the eyes, but it's another story when you come face to face with the "through sickness and health" vow that is sure to come between two people sooner …or later.

Chapter 5

Ivy recalled the moment she walked out of the shower and Jack looked heartbroken at the sight of her beaten body. She knew then how foolish she had been for thinking that sickness would have separated them. This man loved her more than the fear of any physical condition and he was proving it minute by minute.

"Had you ever been ill before in this relationship?" Dr. Gilbert asked.

"A few times," Ivy admitted, "But even those times I tried to hide it from Jack. Not that I was successful in hiding. Jack always knows when something isn't right whether I confessed it or not," she laughed. "He would say, 'I'm not crazy girl I know you and I know when something is wrong with you'," Ivy said, shaking her head

"Why would you try hide sickness from the man you love?"

"I was afraid," Ivy confessed.

"Afraid of?"

Ivy shared with Dr. Gilbert how she had been abandoned in past relationships during times of sickness. It scared her to let Jack know she was sick and risk him not be willing to care for her if that's what she needed.

"So in this moment you were sure that your doubt in his commitment was foolish?" said Dr. Gilbert.

"In that particular moment, I was sure. He was really overwhelmed with concerned he was ready to take me right back to the hospital if anything was wrong. But I assured him that I would be okay. Especially with him there with me. But then, of course, he told me he had to leave."

"To go to D.C."

"Right."

"And how did you feel?"

"I was a little irritated, but then I knew his job was still his job and, if going out there would mean that this particular case would finally be closed forever, then I would be a grown-up about it."

Ivy remembered how Jack carefully helped her put on her pajamas, which was a different experience in that he was much more familiar with taking clothes off of her. In that moment, as he walked her into the

44

living room, he was so honored to be the man that could take care of her this way. Her mother met them in the room and brought in her medicine and some water as she got as comfortable as she could.

"Okay, Jack," Ivy said, finally responding to the news of his departure.

"Okay?"

"I understand babe, plus Mommy and Kayla will be with me so I will be okay." Mother Kasey and Kayla both co-signed and assured Jack that everything would be okay. He continued to give them all the details of the upcoming trip. He wasn't going to ever make the mistake of not be completely honest ever again. As he was talking Ivy was falling asleep. She couldn't help it. The medication was doing just what it was supposed to.

Ivy explained to Dr. Gilbert, "By the time I woke up the next morning, he was gone."

"And you hated it," Dr. Gilbert declared. She knew it was about time Ivy admitted she just didn't like Jack's job.

"Hate is a pretty strong word..."

"So what do you feel about his job?"

"I ..." she paused. "Jack loves his job so I ..."

"Ivy. There's no need to waste your time here being dishonest. You have every right to feel what you feel. How do you feel about Jack's job?"

Thin trickles of tears began to flow from her eyes. Ivy's already glowing skin was magnified under each pocket of water falling on her face as she tried to figure out how to say what she had been dreading to say out loud.

"I hated it. I didn't like it at all!" she cried with all sincerity. "And I hate even more how bad I feel about saying that."

"Why do you feel bad? You're not saying you hate Jack, you're only admission is that you don't care for his professional career."

"But what he does is so meaningful to everyone. It's honorable and I admire him so much, but here I am, angry that he's dedicated to a life of service?" This is why Ivy tried so hard not to complain. She didn't know how to tell Jack how much it hurt when he was late, or didn't show up, or just forgot completely that there were other things going on. How could she complain when so many benefitted from his dedication?

"Your anger is not about his life of service but about the lack of balance and boundaries. Do you talk about those or argue about them?"

"No... we don't argue."

"Why not?"

Ivy sighed.

"Because for Jack, I'm his safe place and if he has to fight with me, then I become just like everything and everyone else that challenges him. So he refuses to argue."

"Challenges are good sometimes. Most of the time challenges let us see how strong we are and force us to rise to meet the next place in life," Dr. Gilbert assured her.

"Jack's work doesn't allow him the grace to accept that kind of thinking. I can accept that, but my work and Jack's work is very different."

Ivy knew that a failure wouldn't define her as a failure. Although being a writer was challenging at times, if she wrote a book or a play that sucked, nobody would get hurt but her.

"If Jack meets a challenge and he fails, and in that failure someone is kidnapped, beaten, and or killed, it's much more difficult to accept challenge as a positive thing," Ivy explained.

"You realize that what happened to you was not a result of failure on Jack's part?"

"Yes, I realize that, but he doesn't. Jack is ..." Ivy paused and laughed. "He's Batman."

"Batman?" Dr. Gilbert questioned with one eyebrow raised. This was her first time hearing something like this. "How do you mean?"

"Trust me I know it sounds weird but it's true. You see... Bruce Wayne was always a good guy, but it was fear of falling victim to the bad guys that created Batman. His life's work became this overwhelming second identity making it very hard for Bruce to ever love and be loved. Jack loves his work. He's identified by the purpose in it and he's married to it. Although most people will never know just how much he does, everyday he's saving lives. But, I was almost a casualty of his dedication and sometimes I think he feels that his love for me makes him weak. Weakness is something he can't afford when there are people's lives at stake. And, like Batman, to avoid giving into the weakness, he'll always find a way to save Gotham, to save the people first, even at the risk of losing what Bruce loves more. And I'm afraid Jack will never let himself love me more than the need to save the world."

"Hmm. I must say Ivy, in my 23 years of this job I have never heard a patient offer such an apt analogy in the discussion of her own case. Not only am I impressed, but I'm kind of jealous that as the Doctor in the room I didn't come up with that."

They both laughed.

"Don't be, it just comes from watching way too many comic book movies, that's all. I've always had a thing for Batman anyway, but I don't know if it's ironic or convenient that my obsession is so accurately applicable to the man I love," Ivy confessed.

"Well, don't sell yourself short, Ivy, that's brilliant." Dr. Gilbert acknowledged.

"Julia, my bachelor's degree is in sociology. I study people on a regular basis because my work as a writer requires me to have the creativity to find the significance in the most juvenile and what may seem ridiculous sort of situations. If I'm going to successfully capture my audience, I have to touch them with the transparency of my own life. I can communicate very eloquently on the pages I write, but having to divulge my true feelings to one person is very challenging. There are plenty of things I know I should have said to Jack, but I simply didn't know how."

Dr. Gilbert didn't worry for Ivy. She felt good that Ivy was admitting her communicational flaws so now it would be easier to help her. The wall was coming down.

"Well, you said something very significant in that Jack was married to the job. A job of which he had before he met you correct?"

"Yes."

"So, you knew this whole time you were a 'mistress'.

"I did."

"So let's talk about why you were okay with being that."

Ivy sighed.

"Like every other mistress, we all believe he'll love us enough to leave his wife," Ivy said. In this case, since Jack wasn't married to an actual woman, but to his career, Ivy believed that eventually he'd realized he was treating her like the "other woman" and reprioritize his life. When he proved unwilling to do so, she had settled for the next place in line. And now she regretted it.

Chapter 6

Dr. Gilbert was now back in session with Jack and he was explaining how Ivy was only home from the hospital for a day and he was leaving her side to answer the call to Washington.

"How did you feel about having to leave her?" Dr. Gilbert inquired.

"I was uncomfortable. I knew she wasn't really happy about me leaving her so soon, but she just pretended to be okay," Jack replied honestly.

"You knew she was pretending?"

"Oh yeah!" Jack replied quickly. "My Sugar is spoiled! And she wants what she wants even if she won't say it. She hates it when I leave her. Most times she acts like it doesn't bother her, but I'm not crazy, I know when she's mad at me. I can feel it."

Dr. Gilbert just smiled.

"Why do you think she pretends? Why wouldn't she just tell you that she wants you to stay?"

"I don't know."

"Maybe she doesn't want to make you choose? Maybe she knows she'll lose and that would hurt more."

Jack leaned back in the chair. "She knows no matter what I have to do she comes first."

"Does she?" Dr. Gilbert was pressing him to really think about if that was really true, but she would move on for now. "So you had to report to Washington. You get there and what happens?"

By 7 o'clock the next morning, Jack was on the ground in Washington, D.C., waiting by the curb for his ride. He only waited a few minutes before agent Forest Kenner was pulling up in the familiar government issued Chevrolet Suburban.

"Good to see you, Detective Benett."

"Is it really?" Jack laughed. Cops don't usually meet because of pleasant situations, so rarely was it a good thing to see one in his mind.

"Anytime you see another cop alive it's good detective."

"You're right about that."

Agent Kenner went over the schedule for the next two days with Jack trying to quickly inform him on FBI protocol. Things were very different at the Federal level. Although Jack was working in the local police department of Rochester, Michigan, he had spent five years in the U.S. Navy so he wasn't completely ignorant on Federal procedure.

"How's your lady, Benett?"

"She's getting better man, thanks for asking. She had a few ribs nearly broken and lots of cuts and bruises, but she and the baby are doing alright."

"That's a strong lady you got there, man."

"Yeah, she's pretty amazing."

"Well, she's a great reason to keep living. So keep on working smart like you did in Cuba and you'll have a long life together. You know the fellas out here were really impressed when they heard how well a rookie worked this case."

"Oh, is that right?"

"Yeah, man."

"I just had a lot on the line that's all. All instincts and prayer man not me."

As they were pulling up to the Federal building Agent Kenner and Detective Benett had both agreed that it had to have been God with them on that island. Things could have gone an entirely different way. Many times in their line of work, the bad guys get away and the innocent wind up dead. They had been blessed.

There weren't many places Jack went into where he felt intimidation, but this was definitely one of them. He felt like small time cop when he entered the conference room at the world headquarters of the Federal Bureau of Investigation. Kenner had told him that he was meeting with the national representatives of narcotics and missing persons, but there were four other men in the room he wasn't expecting. One gentleman in particular looked oddly familiar, but he didn't know why. He did recognize immediately that this was no mere meeting to close a case. These guys had something else up their sleeves.

It was the familiar looking gentleman that stood first to introduce himself. He stood tall, buttoning up his suit coat and walking toward Jack with an odd grin on his face.

"Detective Benett, I'm Senior Agent James Kasey. Have a seat."

As he met the gentleman's hand, Jack was in shock as he realized he was shaking hands with Ivy's father.

"Whoa!" Julia exclaimed, "That had to be a real shock."

"Oh yeah! I was not prepared for that at all. Especially since I was right about them wanting more from me then information about the case. They were offering me a job and her father would be my direct supervisor."

"Wow! How did that come about?"

Kenner was right about the bureau being impressed. They had been watching Jack very closely and once they learned that his girlfriend was Agent Kasey's daughter, the microscope got much bigger. Now it made even more sense that they had gotten so heavily involved in this case.

"You look confused Detective," Agent Kasey said matter-of-factly, "What's the problem?"

"What's the problem? You all called me away from my very delicate fiancé to offer me a job? This couldn't have waited until we got our lives back on track?" Jack was heated! Not only did he have his own reservations about this man, due to his lack of presence in his daughter's life, but it seemed he was even more inconsiderate than Jack thought possible. Agent Kasey, sensing the young officer's discontent decided, to clear the room.

"Let us have the room, gentlemen," Agent Kasey said with his eyes still focused on Jack.

Every other officer and agent in the room got up and left quietly and Agent Kenner closed the door behind them. James Kasey was not a man to beat around a bush, but in this case he took full advantage of his upper hand and circled around Jack like a bird of prey. He slowly took a seat right in front of Jack, who was not at all intimidated at this point and so didn't flinch.

"I take it my daughter hasn't said much about me?"

"In the last almost two years we've been together you haven't said much to her. I wouldn't expect her to have a lot to say," Jack stated with plenty attitude.

"You have a smart mouth to be so far out of your league, Jack Benett."

"With all due respect, Agent Kasey, I didn't come looking for you, so I think I'm entitled to my attitude seeing as how you called me away from more important things. Most importantly, your daughter, whom I would think you would be more concerned about."

James Kasey laughed and shook his head. "How arrogant this kid must be", he thought.

"My daughter is the only reason why you're here Detective! You think the FBI sends special agents and choppers out for every single kidnapping that occurs in the U.S.? Even though we would like to, we don't even have that kind of man- power! Everything you got to help you solve that case was because I ordered it! It was all for my daughter's safety and happiness so don't think for one second it all came together because you're just that good of a cop!"

Although shocked to now know the truth about the matter, Jack wasn't about to let this man tell him he wasn't good at what he does.

"Regardless of what you did from your desk, when your daughter was about to drown into the Atlantic Ocean where were you? I couldn't care less how much work you did from out here, you still have me to thank for your daughter's life, sir!" Jack made sure to emphasize his position so there was no mistake in who was actually there to save Ivy's life. "Now, you didn't bring me out here just to insult me as a man or as an officer so I must have done something right. Why don't we get to what that is so I can go home to be with my family?"

"Alright, Jack."

James Kasey was definitely impressed. Jacks posture in that room had only confirmed that he had found the right man for the job. So without any more antics of testing, Agent Kasey went on to inform Jack of why he was in Washington.

The FBI indeed wanted to hire Detective Benett to head up a special project. Agent Kasey was the Chief of the Safe Streets and Gang unit for the FBI. They were putting together a joint task force of local, state, and federal agencies whose priority would be to deter, detect, and neutralize gang and drug related activity in Mid-Michigan with a heavy concentration in the Flint area. The federal government had no choice at this point, but to step in before Flint and Saginaw were taken over by Marshal Law. The violence was outstanding and now with so many children falling victim to it, the FBI was determined to put a stop to it.

For over 20 years Agent Kasey worked in law enforcement in the Flint area and, although he had moved into the national arena, he had not forgotten his hometown. There were still some very important people there that he wished to protect and this was his first big effort in doing so. Placing Jack over this project would not only mean he had a guy in there he could trust, but he could be sure his daughter was very well taken care of. This job would almost triple Detective Benett's current salary, which would mean the pregnant Ivy, could be still for a change and deliver a healthy grandbaby with no worries of money-making.

Jack was quite surprised with this offer that sat before him. He, too, had a strong desire to put to rest the ridiculous number of murders occurring in the city, but hadn't found how to do it. Internally, the Flint and Detroit Police Departments were corrupt and poor and that's how he ended up working in Rochester. This was definitely an incredible opportunity, but to head a project like this looked like it required much more experience than he thought he had.

"Sir, I've only been a cop for eight years. There are plenty of other guys with more experience than I have. This is not a job I want to be responsible for screwing up."

"I have your resume already, Benett. You would've already been a lot further in your career if it wasn't for your nephew being kidnapped." Agent Kasey said as he released a Jack's file onto the table. He opened it up to find every piece of information possible that the government had on him from his first mug shot at 15 to his test scores for becoming a detective.

"I know how many years you've been in the department, kid. I also know that you spent time in jail yourself for a weapon related misdemeanor that you were lucky didn't stay on your record. But, you got smart. Got off the streets and enlisted in the Navy and became a Seal! We only have 2500 active Seals in the United States and you were one of them and one of the best, according to our records. That's a hell of a lot stronger than Army strong Benett. You're sharp, Jack, and you're young enough to still have the passion it's going to take to get the job done. That's why I need you to lead this team."

The FBI had indeed been looking at the young detective for quite some time to know his record. Jack had not even told Ivy that he was in fact a Navy Seal. That's next level military with special skills some men wish they didn't have.

James Kasey handed him another folder with the details of the assignment. It would move him into Flint, where the base of operations would be, and it included a very high starting salary. This would completely change his career plans and he was already in the middle of major changes. He was now a full-time father of a toddler and engaged to the mother of his growing second child. Jack wasn't sure if this was the right time for this kind of career move.

"Don't answer just yet Benett. Take some time and think about it. You can't discuss it with anybody in your local department but you can talk it over with Ivy. Pray, do whatever you need to do to get your answer to 'yes' Detective. Missing persons in a local station isn't the place for you kid. You're FBI. You have until 9 a.m. next Monday to agree with me."

Agent Kasey called in Agents Kenner and Washington and instructed them to take Detective

Benett back to the airport. He was released to go home to his fiancé.

Chapter 7

"You wake up next morning and Jack's gone. How were you feeling?" Dr. Gilbert continued with Ivy.

"I was really better than I thought I'd be. My mom was there, Kayla was there and so I was okay."

Ivy woke up to the pleasant smell of her mother cooking breakfast. A nice large bottle of water was sitting on the table next to her morning medication. She was extremely thirsty drinking almost twice as much water as she normally did. The baby must have been a fish like she was. After finishing the entire 32 ounces of water, Ivy leaned back and smiled as she laid her hand on her belly. It had been struggle at first but now she was totally engaged in the joy of being pregnant and was determine to love every moment.

"Why was it a struggle at first?"

"At the time I realized I could be pregnant Jack and I weren't together. I was under the impression that he and Lisa had reunited and so the thought of having his baby without him was painful."

"What were you going to do before you knew the truth?"

"I was going to move back to Florida. I wasn't going to tell Jack. I was just going to go."

"You weren't going to tell Jack that he was having a baby?"

"I was under the impression that he had made his choice, and seeing as how I wasn't, it I thought leaving would be the best thing."

"And you didn't want to be in the same shoes Lisa had been in after Jack had chosen you?" Dr. Gilbert stated the honest truth that Ivy was fearful to admit. She couldn't get away with it with someone who knew what she was doing. She had decided to be a coward and Julia called her on it.

"I know it was selfish... but I was heartbroken. I thought I was the love of his life and to call home to find out Lisa was living with him was too much. I didn't know how to face that."

"At least you can admit that Ivy. I've found that when we make selfish decisions like that, it's a sign that we lack confidence in what we thought sure to be right. It's important that we have enough trust and patience to wait for clarity before we commit. When did you find out for sure that you were pregnant?"

"After I woke up in the hospital. It took a couple days to sink in because I had been in and out of consciousness and they weren't sure if I would make it."

"So the truth is out now. You know Lisa had lied and the whole time Jack was very much still in love with you and you're engaged! Why wasn't there any talk about the wedding?"

When her thoughts should be on her wedding Ivy was finding herself thinking much more about baby names, morning sickness and labor. The wedding was minor at this point. Ivy would be perfectly fine saying her vows in the pastor's office and being done with it. Her main concern was the growing miracle inside her.

"So my mom walks into the living room with a tray full of food." Ivy's appetite had decreased quite a bit, but she forced herself to eat for the sake of the baby. Her mother helped her get to the recliner so she could eat comfortably.

"Mommy, this is way too much food."

"Oh hush, child, and eat. When you eat well, your baby comes out with a pretty smile."

"Ma where you get that from?" Ivy laughed as she ate a spoonful of sweet, buttery grits.

"It's true, that's what the old folks say. I ate real well and look how pretty you turned out." They both laughed and Ivy continued to eat.

"Where's Kayla?"

"Right here," moaned a very tired Kayla. She had her hands full of bridal books, magazines and her planner. It was time to work. Ivy was her Maid of Honor and was kind of glad to have so much time off to focus on her cousins wedding.

Kayla and Tank weren't planning anything big and spectacular. They only wanted close friends and family present, but Kayla was very specific on the details of her ceremony that were a must. They were having what Ivy had affectionately nicknamed, A Love Musical. It was going to be like an adult version of High School Musical with the most romantic and sentimental love songs they could find to describe their journey of falling in love. The wedding party was pretty much a cast of amazing singers and musicians that were about to rock out in a very romantic way. This was Ivy's first time producing/coordinating a wedding and of course she intended perfection.

Music was such a huge part of their lives and it is what brought Kayla and Tank together, along with the rest of the band. When they met during one of Ivy's shows in Dallas, they were immediately attracted to one another, but it took them a couple years to come together. Once they did, it didn't take long for things to move swiftly. In six months they were engaged and six months after was the wedding date. They were only two months away now, but due to the recent tour and madness with Ivy, they were all involved with, they had missed quite a few weeks of planning. They were about to make up for it as much as they could this week.

Kayla and Ivy would spend all day finalizing details of the wedding. It was the best distraction for Ivy while Jack was away. She was slightly worried because he hadn't called, but when she woke up, she had a text from him confirming that he had made it safely and that he loved her. It was all she had and she repeatedly looked at that same text and smiled.

"How many times are you going to look at that text girl?" Kayla teased.

"Over and over again honey!" Ivy laughed.

"You so silly. So you thinking about a date for your big day? You know this is a big deal right?"

"How is my wedding any more of big deal than yours?"

"I'm not an illustrious bachelorette like you, Ivy," Kayla joked. "You've had five proposals, accepted two, and called both of them off. This is my first, only and last! You know everybody is on pins and needles to see if this one you'll actually go through with. You kind of have this runaway bride thing happening."

Kayla was joking, of course, but she did have a point. In the past, Ivy had been very indecisive with her heart and was well aware of her commitment issues. All of that went out of the window with Jack. There was no doubt in her mind that he was God's man for her life. She was very excited about becoming his wife, but wedding plans weren't bringing her any welcomed anxieties. It was enough right now just to know she was very sure of her heart for the first time in a very long time.

"Wait... let's pause for a moment," Julia interrupted, "You've had five proposals, accepted two, and called them both off?"

"That is correct," Ivy laughed. "It's not as bad as it sounds, I promise. It wasn't the men as much as it was me and my fear of commitment."

"I don't think it sounds bad, I think it's interesting that you have recognized that those were results of your commitment issues. Most often we talk about men stalling in that department and I must say it's nice to hear women admit this problem and take the responsibility for it. What was so different about Jack?"

Ivy smiled. "He was stronger than me."

"How do you mean?"

"One thing that was on the top of my list when I prayed about my husband was being secure. I wanted more than anything to be protected. I wanted a man that would keep me safe and not just physically safe, even though that was a part of it."

"Yes, that's understandable. That's not an odd request. Was strength something you had lacking in past relationships?"

"Well, it wasn't that the men weren't strong. They just weren't strong enough," Ivy said shaking her head. "They were always doing too much to try to prove they could keep a woman like me in check and I didn't need that."

"What do you mean, a 'woman like me'? Like what exactly?"

"Working for myself means that I'm always having to make the tough decisions. I have to be in charge. So I admit sometimes it wasn't easy to release that control when I went into a relationship. Most times I didn't want to because I didn't trust them."

Ivy admitted to becoming great at things because of having to do them herself. Everything wasn't just pure talent. Lots of things were just hard work. She learned the hard way that even the best people can let you down so you have to know how to do things yourself. Building that kind of strength had made her a stubborn workaholic and afraid to let others help for fear they would let her down.

"So I found myself dating men that I knew weren't going to stop me from doing what I wanted to do. By the time I had tired of the relationship, and was ready to show them the door, I wasn't going to have missed a beat."

"So why was it necessary to need strength if you weren't going to let it be?"

"Because I was scared ...and selfish. I promised myself that nobody was going to carry me away with love because that would give them the power to drop me in mid-air. Before Jack I didn't know how to fly."

"Aha... Good metaphor! So what could Jack do that they couldn't?"

Ivy paused and just looked out of the window as if she was trying to collect the right words to answer such a question. There was so much that Jack did for her that had never been done. She wasn't really sure how to verbalize it and make it make sense.

"Jack could protect me from even myself. When I'm doing too much and don't realize it, he can spot it and stop me and I listen to him. The other men wouldn't notice until it was too late. Not because they didn't care, but they didn't see what he did. Jack knows that I am the ultimate danger to myself and that my greatest strength is also my greatest weakness."

"Hmm..." Dr. Gilbert quickly jotted some notes down and looked at her watch. "We'll get further into that at another time. Let's go back to this assurance that you had that Jack was it for you. It's clear that your family and possibly others had some doubts, but those weren't because of Jack, they were because of you."

"Right, so I told Kayla that they could all stop wondering because Jack was the one."

"Oh, I know he is," Kayla said confidently. "But just a heads up… Curtis isn't convinced yet."

"Yeah, I know," Ivy regrettably confessed to Kayla. She knew it was her fault that Curtis had no peace with her decision to marry Jack, but she knew how to handle it.

The band had been a safety zone for Ivy over the last five years and had brought her so much joy. She felt such a strong sense of purpose when they got on that stage together, but her purpose had been redirected to Jack and the baby and that was going to take precedence over the music. Jack was her safe place now and to ensure she didn't allow any negativity to enter that space she would have to make some very tough decisions. The first and toughest decision was to leave the band.

"I hadn't shared it with Kayla just yet but I knew what I had to do," Ivy shared with Dr. Gilbert.

"Why did you think leaving the band was the best thing to do? Music seems to be such a big part of who you are. Why were you so ready to give that up?"

"It wasn't so much that I was ready to give up music, but that I was realizing my limitations. Like I said, my relationship with Jack and our family was my priority."

"Was this your decision?"

"Yes, it was mine. I wasn't entirely happy about what I would lose, but I was more excited about what I would be gaining. I meant it when I told Curtis that I had made my choice."

"So deciding to leave your music was part of your attempt to prove that."

"Yes."

"Are you satisfied with that decision? Did it help you move forward?"

"What I can say is that it taught me a valuable lesson."

"Which was?"

Ivy looked down and rubbed the engagement ring that was kind of snug now on her chubby finger. As she twisted it back and forth she muttered slowly, "You'll always have something or someone to give up if you're going to move forward and, even when it's the right thing to do, you won't always be left feeling satisfied."

Chapter 8

"That was nice of Agent Kasey to let you come home early," Dr. Gilbert said to Jack.

"I guess you could call it that. I was just glad to be able to get home" Jack confessed.

It was around ten o'clock in the evening when he arrived back in Rochester from D.C. He wasn't really tired but still very much in shock from the meeting with Ivy's father and being offered such an incredible job. There were so many decisions to make and he wasn't going to make them alone. Now he had so much more to consider than himself. With the keys in his hand, standing at the door, he prepared to go inside his lady's home and share with her the details of his trip.

The house was quiet. He carefully walked into the living room as not to startle Ivy knowing that she would be sound asleep. He grinned when he saw her cuddled up in her grandmother's blanket. She was sleeping so peacefully in the Lay-Z-Boy he had bought for her. Jack stood there for a moment and just looked at her. The one good thing about this job offer was that it would keep him inside of an office and off of the streets so he had less worry about not returning home to this angel. He could finally be the family man he always desired and provide very well for his home.

"So you wanted to take the job?" Dr. Gilbert asked.

"For that reason alone, yes. I thought if I could make it home by a certain time every day it would be much more stable for us and our growing family."

"At least that was the plan," said Julia.

"That was the plan."

"Continue…"

"So I leaned down and kissed her face. She always did this thing when she was sleep that was so cute. She rarely snored and if she did I knew something was wrong, but she hummed in her sleep," Jack said, smiling.

"Did I sleep the whole week or are you home early?" mumbled Ivy, half awake.

"I'm home early."

"Prove it," she demanded in a whisper, "Kiss me again."

Of course, he did as she asked. He leaned down in front of her and kissed her lips until she was completely awake and responding intensely to the movement of his lips. She slowly pushed the footrest back and sat up. Jack wrapped her up in his arms and hugged her gently. He sat back onto the coffee table in front of her and held her hands. Looking at the engagement ring that was sitting comfortably on her left hand, he thought intensely of the life he was now able to promise her. Although Ivy was loving this extra affection that he was now showing her, she knew there was something more to it.

"Extra affection? Was affection something new to her?" Julia asked.

"Not really new, but it was just a lot more of it," Jack replied.

"Naturally, because of what happened you were feeling like you needed to make sure she knew how much she meant to you."

"Yeah, I mean, it wasn't as if before I didn't show her attention, but I was just more reserved."

"Why?"

"Well, at first it was because we weren't having sex and I was trying to hold out. So I couldn't handle being all over her all the time and not be getting any. I wasn't strong enough for that."

"So then what happened after you started having sex?"

"I was still reserved. We both struggled with having sex before marriage because we just weren't raised that way. Of course, that didn't stop me, but I was holding back. I hadn't given her all of me. After almost losing her it was easy to be affectionate even without going all the way. She was too weak for sex, but I still needed to be near her and to touch her and hold her."

Ivy knew Jack well and knew the abundant affection was due to the changes they had gone through. Although she welcomed it, she knew something was up.

"What's with you Jack?" Ivy grinned.

"What do you mean?"

"I mean what happened in D.C.? Is everything good?"

"Yeah, Lady, everything is fine. Really fine actually. I was offered a job," he confessed.

"What kind of job? Will you have to leave?" Ivy worried instantly. Any government job could mean separation and distance that could prove fatal to a good relationship. Her father was her proof.

"No, no, no, not leaving you," Jack assured her. "If I take the job we would have to move, but I'm not going anywhere without you." Jack went on to share with her the details of the job and how much of a raise it would be, not only financially, but he would move swiftly up the ladder in his career working directly with the FBI. Ironically, this kind of move was the same that Lisa was trying to pressure him into. It looked different now and because of Ivy, it was much more meaningful.

Ivy placed both hands on Jacks face and with her head leaned to side she smiled and said,

"Jack… you are the love of my life. I will go with you anywhere."

Jack just smiled and shook his head.

"Thank you, Sugar."

Not that he ever questioned her loyalty but Jack was very glad to be reassured that she was in support of whatever decision he made. He knew he still had to share that her father was the man that wanted to hire him, but that could wait.

"Sugar?" Dr. Gilbert questioned. "That was new... you had been calling her 'Lady' before then. What was with the name change?" she asked, as she was taking notice of lots of small things Jack hadn't planned on explaining. Not that it was difficult, but because some things he himself hadn't even noticed he was doing.

"You know... she just seemed so much sweeter to me than before." He grinned and shook his head as he thought of her. Jack was comforted by the memory of what she had been to him. "She's my Sugar," Jack repeated before getting back to the story.

He had looked down again at Ivy's left hand.

"Do you know when I bought this ring?"

"No," Ivy replied.

"You remember the night we first got busy?" he said jokingly. Ivy laughed.

"Baby, don't say 'got busy'", blushed the prim Ivy.

"Okay, okay, I'm playing. The first time I made love to you? And I say, when *I* made love to *you* because you really couldn't do too much. You weren't ready for me," he teased.

"Will you stop it?" she laughed.

"Okay, okay, do you remember, is the question?" Jack didn't have to ask he already knew she remembered and that there was no way on God's precious green earth that she could forget that night.

Like many times before Jack had come to spend the evening watching movies with his little lady in his arms. Nothing about this night seemed to be any different than before. They cuddled up on her sofa on which they had fallen asleep on together many times before over those past six months. It had been a very long day for them both and although they were tired they were comforted to be with each other. Ivy was used to giving so much of herself to work and family, but, when Jack held her she was restored.

Her eyes were closed. She drifted off to sleep thinking about how she had ever survived without his love. Jack, however, although elated he had Ivy to end his days with, did not want to sleep that night. He wanted her. His usual tactic of relaxing her and putting her to sleep was softly rubbing her ears and just like every other night, it had worked. But the moment Ivy turned into his chest and buried herself in his strong arms, something moved in Jack that he could no longer fight. He gently rubbed her back, then slowly eased his warm hand down her side, gripped her wide hip and pulled her leg up over his hip leaving no space in between them.

Ready to fulfill every fantasy he had ever had since the first night he met her, Jack could not wait any longer. He lightly kissed her awake. Though Ivy had always melted into his kisses she knew this one was meant to seal his name on her heart. She knew he was strong, but didn't realize how truly strong he was until he lifted her up and gently laid her back down underneath him just the way he wanted her. With his body positioned perfectly between her legs, Jack looked into her eyes, told Ivy he loved her and that she was the last woman he ever wanted to kiss.

His lips touched hers with so much purpose that time itself seemed to stand still. There wasn't much between his hands and her body as she was only wearing a thin, black, caftan-like dress that she only wore for relaxing at home. It was easy for Jack to glide his strong hands underneath the thin material and remove the purple seamless panties that graced her ample backside. He made her lose herself in his kisses so much so she couldn't recall in her mind how, minutes later, she was free of all clothing that once covered her entire body. Her little brown hands seemed even smaller as she tried with all her strength to grip the sharp, meaty blades of his coffee colored back as he gently thrust himself into her.

Usually, Ivy was so much in control during sex. She knew what was happening and was present in every moment but with Jack, that moment that felt like forever. She was lost. Jack made love to her so passionately that it brought tears to her eyes. Those tears represented such unexpected pleasure and the joyful erasing of every memory of the lovers of her past. The sun was rising through the beige curtains in her window when he kissed her soft brown shoulder as she drifted off to sleep.

"Yes, of course, I remember that night," Ivy admitted grinning.

"Well, that next day I went and bought this ring" Jack confessed. After that night there was no doubt in his mind that this was his wife. God wouldn't have it any other way. He had kept it hidden for eight months. There had been so many times when he planned to propose, but it seemed everything kept getting in the way. When things would calm down for him at work, she would be on the road with her work. Of course, Lisa had been a constant nightmare as well.

With all the craziness their petty arguing had begun to erupt into more drama that Jack admitted stemmed from his inability to trust her completely. He was unconsciously making Ivy pay for the damage that Lisa had done and that almost caused him to lose her.

"You knew you had a lack of trust?" Dr. Gilbert asked, bringing him back into the present.

"Yeah…"

"Had she ever done anything even remotely reminiscent of the behaviors that you dealt with in your relationship with Lisa?"

"Only that she wanted to argue."

"And you didn't?"

"Not at all. I mean I knew she didn't want to fight the same way Lisa did, but it was still an argument and I didn't want to get into with her."

"You know arguing is not always a bad thing? In fact it's necessary if we're going to gain understanding we need to talk and sometimes our tones may elevate, but, as long as we're not hitting below the belt, it's a healthy process."

"I didn't want to argue with her," he stated firmly. Jack meant what he said.

"Why not?"

"I'm challenged on almost every part of my job on a daily basis. I don't want to come home and be challenged there, too!" Jack said, not realizing he was raising his voice. "She was the only safe place I had. If I have to argue with her, then it's just like being at work with everyone else who I have to prove myself to everyday!"

"I do understand the necessity for having a safe place, but we have a responsibility to guard our safe places with compassion and understanding. She needs a safe place, too. If when Ivy needed that and she couldn't get it from you, then she's left without the very thing you needed from her. It creates an unhealthy imbalance that's not safe for either of you. What could be a peaceful conversation to gain understanding will no doubt become an ongoing fight and eventually no one wants to apologize or move forward. That's how you all got here."

Jack knew that was exactly the space they were in now. Too many fights that could have been talks, they've both stop listening and no one wants to admit they were wrong. Dr. Gilbert was working to get them both the see the value in what they once had and that it's very much worth holding on to. She had reminded Jack that this time he had just acknowledged he had let too much get in the way of what was good.

"Now that you had put all that behind you and committed to love and trust her, what was next?"

"There was one thing I had left to do correctly," Jack said calming down. "I slipped the ring off of her finger and got down on my knee." He didn't get a chance to do this the way he had planned and realized that none of his plans mattered.

"I know I asked you in that hospital room to be my wife but I'm asking again to make sure it wasn't just the medication that made you say yes."

Ivy laughed.

"Ivy Lynn Kasey, I have no desire to spend the rest of my life with anyone, but you. Will you marry me?"

A silent Ivy had tears streaming down her chubby brown cheeks. She had been very heavily medicated and in and out of consciousness in that hospital and hadn't remembered all the details of his first proposal. Now, here at home, it was all real. This was the proposal she had dreamt about, wrote about and acted out many times before, but never thought it would be her reality. She wrapped her arms around Jack's neck and as she cried she whispered a quiet, but very sincere 'yes' into his ear. As she cried in his arms she thanked God for making her wait so long for this moment. It was worth it.

Jack enjoyed her embrace, but he had just one more surprise in mind for his Sugar. She slid back into her chair as he slipped the ring back onto her finger.

"I know we said we didn't want to add the stress of wedding planning right now, but I'm not moving you anywhere without my last name. I want to do everything right from now on."

"Jack, I'm perfectly okay with moving in with mommy until the wedding."

"No, I want you with me."

"Ok, so what do you want to do?"

"What about something private and simple... at the end of the month?"

"This month?!"

"Yes, this month. We'll rent a house up north, with just a few people. Then, later on, after the baby is born, we can have a big reception for the rest of our family and friends."

Ivy was used to Jack's impulsive nature by now. It used to be so unsettling because she didn't like surprises and he was so unpredictable, but a private wedding in a lodge up north sounded just perfect.

"Okay."

"Yeah?" Jack wasn't so sure she would go for it. Her family was very traditional and many will feel some kind of way about an 'elope' style wedding. Then again, he knew his Lady had the potential to be a wild card, so it was settled. Jack and Ivy were getting married on Saturday, October 29th, only three weeks away.

Chapter 9

Ivy needed to get up and walk around for a bit, she began to feel her legs tightening as she was sitting there with Dr. Gilbert. With her dress dragging the floor, she walked back and forth in that office and continued to talk about what she remembered when Jack came home from D.C.

"I remember feeling like I was dreaming. I knew part of it was just how loopy the medicine made me, but I was really surprised that he was home so early."

"Happy surprised?"

"Of course!" she smiled. "We both knew I hadn't really wanted him to go, but you know he had to work. I wasn't as excited when he told me about that job offer."

"Yes, this is the job that moved you two back here into Flint where you were raised. What did you think about that?"

The more Jack had talked about it, and its possibilities, the more Ivy could tell that he wanted to take the job although he was apprehensive in asking her about moving back.

"Like many other people that grew up in Flint, when I left I swore I would never go back. Not because I hated it, but there was just so much more in the world I had experienced that made Flint seem too small to settle into."

That was before she knew where life would take her. She had family in Flint most importantly her mother, and she was about to be a new mother. Ivy would need her Mommy. Not to mention she could do her work from anywhere and this was an awesome opportunity for her man to live out his dream.

"So there was no question to what you would do." Dr. Gilbert implied.

"Not at all. It was a great opportunity for him and I wanted to support him. He would have a different kind of work so I thought it would cut down the amount of time he had to be on the job, which was a plus for us."

"It didn't take any convincing for you then?" Julia laughed.

"Nah," Ivy admitted. "Plus, he was so gooey acting it was kind of cute."

"What do you mean?"

"He was so much more affectionate than he was before the incident. He was kissing me all the time, holding my hand, rubbing my arms or my face. He was always touching me in some way. It was so funny," Ivy laughed.

"Why was that funny to you?"

"Not funny in a bad way, but like 'funny cute' you know?" She placed her hands on her hips and stood still shaking her head. Ivy looked at Dr. Gilbert in the face and continued. "Jack was never one for public displays of affection. Especially in the beginning because he respected my efforts to abstain from sex, which was hard for us both. When he couldn't stand it, he would just not come around me to avoid being close. Once I understood that, I wasn't offended because, although I'm more of a touchy feely girl, it was sometimes too much for me to be near him and not be able to have him, if you know what I mean."

"I do understand," she laughed. "So what about afterwards?"

"Well... I could tell that he was still kind of holding back a little. I don't know why he was, but I was okay with that at that time."

"You just said that you enjoyed affection so why were you okay knowing he was holding back?"

"Okay, Julia, listen, one thing between Jack and I that was perfect was the P.O.I!" Suddenly everything about Ivy's tone changed and Dr. Gilbert was quickly noting every change in her personality.

"Excuse me, your poi? As in the staple of Polynesian food?" Julia asked.

Ivy laughed.

"No, I'm sorry Julia, let me explain. You know I teach workshops from time to time on personal development?"

"Yes, we talked about it briefly over the phone," Julia remembered.

"Okay, well one of the more exclusive ones is called *The P.O.I.* which stands for the *Power of Intimacy*. It's designed mainly for the spiritual woman to help her become confident and totally secure in her sexuality so that she can maintain a healthy and more so enjoyable sex life with her husband."

"That sounds awesome and so very necessary for the Christian community! How did you get to that when you come from such a conservative upbringing?" Julia inquired.

"Well, I got to it actually because of my conservative upbringing," Ivy laughed. "Sex was almost a curse word growing up and it seemed like there was never an appropriate time and place to talk about it. When it was talked about it in our young adult groups it was such a hell and damnation sort of conversation that it was hard to get the truth out of the whole thing. This is what God gave me. I wanted women to understand that intimacy was so much more than sex and, once we get that, our sex gets so much better," Ivy said honestly.

The truth was that once she discovered how absolutely amazing sex was she couldn't understand why people acted like it was so bad. She wished someone would have been honest enough to just say it's fabulous and God made it that way, but here are the reasons why you should wait, why you should be careful and why you should be wise.

Ivy also realized how damaging it was that so many married women in the church were misunderstanding the difference in conservative and lady-like and an insecure prude. The continued circulation of very poor advice resulted in too many women believing that sex was only for their husband, which was why so many were ignorantly too quick to stop giving it up. She wanted to rectify that problem. Ivy wanted to help women be bold and confident enough in their own skin to go home and get butt-naked with their husbands and enjoy it!

"So I had no problem being transparent in the bedroom and neither did Jack. He was present, he was focused, he was attentive, and …. I mean I'm not stupid I know every man fantasizes no matter how much he's in love, but I just knew he was with me. I also knew that there was more physically that he was capable of, but he wasn't going to release it."

"And that was fine with you?"

"Yes! I wasn't ready for all of him in that way. I was already in love with Jack before he ever kissed me, if he had given me everything, I'd really be coo-coo for Cocoa Puffs right now."

Julia belted out a laugh so intense it made Ivy laugh at herself. She was loosening up now and Julia could see more of who she was as her comedic character began to surface.

Dr. Gilbert took a deep breath, "Whew! Now that was funny. Okay so Jack's back early and you're excited to see him. He's all 'lovey-dovey' and has the opportunity to take a great new job. Then what?"

"Then, he surprises me by proposing to me again and setting an immediate date for the wedding!" Ivy was looking at the ceiling and she was shaking her hands back and forth like she was confused.

"Were you overwhelmed?"

"I really was… it was so much all at once. The baby, his daughter, trying to recover, leaving the band, being engaged and now, getting married and having to move." She said all in one breathe. Ivy slowly took a deep breath and exhaled slowly. "I was so happy… but it was overwhelming because I wasn't sure why he wanted to move so fast."

"Did you ask him?"

"No," she admitted sitting back down on the couch. "I didn't ask, I went right along with it. I mean... I was finally getting everything I wanted. Why ask questions?"

Dr. Gilbert did understand Ivy's resolve to just go along with the flow instead of asking questions. Why tamper with what seems to be perfection? Meanwhile, Ivy had friends and family that were very concerned for her and couldn't know the truth. Julia needed to know what they're perspective of the situation was. She needed to know how Ivy's family was contributing her feelings of being overwhelmed.

"What was your family thinking about all this?" Julia asked.

"Well, they had been told that I was in a boating accident while we were in Cuba. Jack and I hadn't been cleared to tell them the truth about what had happened. My sisters had come over to talk me about being still for a while knowing my tendency to overdo it."

Ivy's family was determined not to overwhelm her or allow her to overwhelm herself. They were still very concerned about how she had planned to move forward with such tremendous changes. She was very much capable of pulling through and they had no doubt about that. There were many other things to consider with all these extreme changes in her life. Ivy was engaged, having a baby and becoming a stepmother to a precious, two-year-old girl. All of this, plus attempting to continue to be a successful entrepreneur, seemed like way too much in the eyes of her siblings. It was their prayer that Ivy would be willing to let some things go.

Ivy's two sisters, Ivory and Ivonne, had come by the house to spend some quality time with their baby sister. Of course, they wanted to ensure that she was obeying doctors' orders, but they were also on a mission to try and make sure Ivy had her priorities in order. They were very ignorant to the details of what she had gone through on that island. As a result they were operating with only limited information. In their minds, this accident she was in, although not her fault, was a result of her overdoing it, as she had so often done in the past.

"What are you two thinking about that's got you all frowned up and looking so sad?" Ivy asked awaking from her nap.

"Hey Sissy, how was your nap?" Ivory asked.

"Thanks to this recliner, sleeping is much easier. Lying flat in that hospital bed was a nightmare. So what are y'all here to talk to me about?"

"What? We can't come and just check on our baby sister?" Ivonne asked with a noticeable smirk on her face.

"Yeah right, don't act brand new," Ivy laughed, "Spill it."

"Well, we are here as your older sisters to pull rank, so to speak," Ivonne admitted.

"Oh yeah? This ought to be good."

"Ivory and I want to make sure that you are not overwhelmed. Nothing is more important right now than you and this baby and so we think some things you may want to think about setting aside for a while."

"I told you all I'm not going to rush back into work. I'm just fine, no worries okay?" Ivy said, trying to calm them.

"But you're not just fine Ivy and we are very worried," Ivory stated sternly. It was time to have a very serious conversation that only her sisters were brave enough to have with her.

"We know how strong you think you are and you are a trooper, we'll give you that, but nobody can do it all. You literally almost died Sissy, and now you're about to be a wife and a full-time mother to, not one, but two children. You travel constantly for work and, I mean, you can't possibly think you can keep this up?" Ivonne sternly interjected.

"We're here to help you put things in perspective. We don't want to get another call that you're lying in a hospital like that ever again! So we've decided that if you don't calm this life down..." Ivory threatened as she looked at Ivy seriously, "We're going to call Boy."

"Boy" was the affectionate nickname of their baby brother, of whom, always got the last word on any situation pertaining to the safety and well-being of his sisters. Especially, Ivy who was the baby. Calling "Boy" carried all the weight Ivy's sisters needed in order to convince her to slow her life down. He was already planning to make a trip up north to check on her, but they didn't need to speed up his plans by telling him that Ivy was being hard-headed.

Ivy sat in her chair looking into the very sincere eyes of her two older sisters and wanted to tell them the truth about what had happened, but it would only raise their concerns. She settled for being able to tell them what they loved to hear, which was that they were absolutely right. Everything about her lifestyle would have to change in order to get acclimated to motherhood and married life. The good news was that she was prepared to do so with a lot less fuss than her sisters were anticipating.

"I appreciate your concerns and I'm happy to tell you that you are right," Ivonne and Ivory looked at each other and then back at Ivy suspiciously.

"We are?" they asked in unison.

Their baby sister was precious indeed, but a spoiled brat with an iron will and rarely did she take kindly to her sisters telling her what to do. They were quite shocked with her response.

"Yes, you're right. My life is going to be very different and, with these new added responsibilities, I have to be even more cautious of unnecessary stress. As much as I love traveling and working, some things that I had my hands in, I will have to give up. I have already committed to working from home until the baby is born and..." she sighed. "I've decided to leave the band." Ivy confessed not having seen that Kayla walked into the room.

"You're doing what?" Kayla yelled.

"Come sit down, Kayla," Ivy asked her calmly. She understood her distress, but needed her to reciprocate the understanding. Although Ivy had been the center of the group, she believed they could carry on without her. More importantly, they didn't have a choice.

Ivy and Curtis had been responsible for putting together an incredible sound, structure of music and lyrics that made it easy for this group of talented people to be successful. They had come to depend on the two of them for every move they made and never thought about the day when Ivy's time with them would be over. Not only was it time consuming, but the dynamic of her relationship with Curtis was only going to change if Ivy induced those changes. They had plenty of amazing adventures and it would all be missed, but when it's time to move, it's time.

"Ivy there is no band without you! You can't leave," Kayla begged. Ivy leaned in and grabbed her hands.

"You guys will be fine. Besides, it's time you stepped into the forefront, Kayla. You're not a background singer. You're a leader and it's time everybody sees that. I'm officially turning it all over to you and with Tank by your side, you guys are going to make magic. You have to trust me… Just don't say anything to everybody yet. I want to be the one to break the news."

As Ivy's sisters got up to fix some food and get her medication, they took the conversation into the kitchen and continued to encourage their cousin, Kayla, and assure her that Ivy's decision was for the best. Even though she still had to talk to the rest of the group, Ivy sat in her chair relieved that she had at least told Kayla about her decision. It would ensure she had the much needed support when she delivered the news to Curtis. Her leaving the group also included Curtis being released from his duties as her producer and manager. To say the least, he would be pissed.

Chapter 10

"Did you know about Ivy's decision to leave her music?" Julia asked Jack.

"Not at the time. She hadn't mentioned it specifically." She had just promised to take things slow."

"How did you feel about her musical career?"

Jack had to think for a minute because the truth was…he hadn't paid that much attention. They met each other because of her work on the stage and in his mind music was only an unnecessary tie to Curtis and he really didn't care for it.

"I didn't really get involved in it. That was kind of just her thing and, because I didn't want to be around Curtis, I kind of ignored the fact that it was something… she liked…doing."

As he said it, he realized how inconsiderate it sounded. He had missed multiple opportunities to support something she loved and he could feel in that moment how that may have made her feel. Dr. Gilbert inquired on what he was experiencing in that moment.

"What are you thinking?"

"I just heard how selfish that was."

"We all have moments of selfishness, Jack. But, to be clear, it wasn't the music you didn't care for. It was who the music kept her close to."

"Right."

"Okay so if we separate Curtis from the music, how do you feel about it?"

Jack smiled. "It's clear I'm a pretty tough guy, but it's hard for me to listen to her sing without tears coming to my eyes," he confessed. "I would record her singing around the house or singing to me at night so when she had to go out of town I could still have her voice with me."

"Did she know you did that?"

"I don't think so."

"What about the rest of her work? Had you read any of her pages? Had you seen any of her plays?"

"I saw one show. The one I met her at. Every other show she had locally I was working those nights. I slipped in to one for a little while when I was working late, but I couldn't stay."

He felt bad, but it wasn't intentional that he wasn't supportive. It just seemed like time moved so fast and before he knew he had missed so much and she never really asked for much.

"Ivy never really asked me to come to stuff. She knew I was busy and I think to avoid me saying I couldn't come she just stopped asking altogether."

"So you admit there was much about her world that you weren't a part of?"

"... I guess so," he hesitantly admitted.

"Outside of the obvious details of your work, were there things in your world that she wasn't a part of? Were there things she didn't support that you wish she had?"

"I can't think of anything she didn't support. I know she didn't care too much for the office parties or the department picnics and softball games, but she would go anyway."

"Why do think she would go?"

"I don't know... I think... maybe she just wanted to be with me," he smiled.

"Why the smile?"

"Because I'm sure that's all she wanted," he paused. "That's why it was so easy to love her, she never wanted anything... just me..."

Dr. Gilbert let that thought sit with Jack for a moment before she moved forward. She knew it was always better when people realized for themselves the reality of their situation. Jack needed to hear himself say and confess these things to remind him of why he loved her and also to help him see ways that he could've loved her better.

"Let me take a detour here, Jack, and ask you this. Were you annoyed sometimes by her loyalty?"

"What's that supposed to mean?" Jack questioned with an attitude. He wasn't comfortable with the insinuation that he felt anything, but love for Ivy.

"It's not an insult, Jack, simply the recognition of a possible truth."

"The truth is and has always been that I love her!"

"And I don't doubt that at all. I know you love her, but I also know that sometimes we can become annoyed by the faithfulness of our partners when we know we're not giving the same amount of support in return. Sometimes, unconsciously, we punish them because we feel incapable of giving at their level," she explained. "The persistent love of the other person, in our eyes, is now only shedding light on our own faults. So we begin to question why they love us at all. And, because now we're feeling undeserving, we do and say really hurtful things to push them away."

It wasn't a direct insult, but it was an acknowledgment of another dynamic that had been happening between the two of them. This was not just on Jack's side, but Ivy was responsible too. It just pained Jack right now because he was the one in the hot seat. Julia went on to explain that these things people do are the unconscious effort of all human beings to protect themselves from pain.

"Jack, you're not being singled out or being labeled a bad person. It's a sign of immaturity in all of us. When maturity comes, we work intentionally to love through and beyond our shortcomings." Dr. Gilbert continued.

"I just feel like I'm running out of ways to prove to her that I love her. Why do I have to work so hard to do that? I mean, I was willing to protect her from her own father!"

"Okay. Tell me about that."

Jack having decided to take the job added some very specific demands on which he would accept. The FBI had already committed to pay for his relocation so he could get started immediately, but Jack wouldn't start until the first week of November. He wanted time to get his family settled. This job would require a lot of hours just in the team building process and he didn't want to have to leave Ivy so swiftly with an entire house to move into and arrange alone. Agent Kasey, of course, understood.

"I do intend to do my best on this job, Agent Kasey, but I want to make sure one thing is very clear sir."

"And what's that, Detective?"

"I appreciate the opportunity, but the second I feel like you or this agency feels like they have me under its thumb or tries to play me like a puppet, I'm done and I do not care what you get left with! My daughter and your daughter are my #1 priority and nothing is going to be worth losing them."

"Relax Benett. I may not be an everyday part of my daughter's life, but she was my baby girl before she was yours. I do love her and this is part of my attempt to make sure she knows that. We're on the same side, son," Agent Kasey responded convincingly. Though Jack believed him, he knew the loyalty of government was conditional. No matter who was in charge there was always another man above him who had the power to change everything.

"With all due respect, sir, as you pointed out, I am a Navy Seal and you know what senses come with that. I ignored all of those, which is what got me into that mess with Lisa. That will never happen again. I'll be sniffing every person on this team, including you."

"I expect nothing less. You're no longer just a detective Jack. You're a Special Agent in the Bureau now."

That was a fact that Jack hadn't really processed. In just two days he had gone from being a local detective to a special agent for the FBI. It was a big leap upward that, he did, in fact owe to Ivy's father.

"I admit I don't understand nor do I want to know all the details of why you and Ivy's relationship is the way it is. I just know I don't want it to affect our marriage which, by the way, will be starting at the end of this month. We're getting married in three weeks and I think you should be there. If she's going to be okay with the job and all in entails, she needs to trust you and right now, she doesn't." Jack said.

Those words hit James Kasey right in his heart simply because they were true. He, of course, didn't like hearing it from Jack, but unfortunately this young rookie knew his daughter a lot better than he did right now. He would have to suck it up and take the heat.

"Okay, Benett. You name the time and place and I'll be there."

"Good. Now if I tell her you're coming and you don't show, don't expect our relationship to be a good one."

"I hear you, Benett."

Jack took a deep breath. He didn't know this man well at all, but his nerve had increased so much over the last month, that he didn't care who he was talking to. There were just some things Jack would no longer do and one of them was placate his true feelings to appease anyone. Even if that someone included his new boss and father in-law to be, Jack wasn't holding his tongue.

"Now that we have that out of the way, Mr. James Kasey I would like to ask for your daughters hand in marriage."

Jack was old school at heart if nothing else. Sure he loathed the idea of the pain this man had cause his daughter, but Jack had no room to judge. In this case, there was still a great deal of hope for Ivy and her dad to get along and Jack would do what was right no matter what.

"If you have the guts to talk to me like that kid, you have my blessing," James responded.

Jack was looking at the wall of books in Dr. Gilbert's office while remembering that conversation.

"I know Ivy's father didn't care too much for my attitude, but I didn't care."

"Why did you feel you needed his approval?" Julia asked.

"Because I knew that he would be a part of our lives and, like I said, I'm still old school, if nothing else, and I wanted to respectfully ask for her hand in marriage."

"You knew this could maybe cause some friction between you and Ivy seeing as how she wasn't on consistent speaking terms with her father."

"I did know that, but I also knew she wanted to have a better relationship with him. If I could be a part of helping her have that then I would."

"At what point did you know that it wouldn't be as easy as just inviting him to the wedding?"

Jack sat quietly trying to pin point the moment he realized bringing Ivy's father into the situation was more complicated than a wedding invitation. He couldn't find it at the moment. So much had happened so quickly and, before he knew it, there wasn't even a wedding for Ivy's father to attend.

Jack muttered, "I don't know," sat back in his chair and folded his arms.

Chapter 11

Ivy was sitting back against the firm pillow on the sofa as the tension in her legs began to cease. Julia's assistant had brought her a stool so that she could elevate those aching feet that so diligently held up the weight of Jack's baby. Ivy and Julia had been discussing the immense amount of planning that had to happen so fast and how that was affecting her. One huge hurdle was allowing Kayla to take over the music and, although it was something Ivy would still love and support, it was no longer her burden. She felt freed of it and it gave her energy to move onto other exciting things.

"So I had gotten up early the next day to start looking for both, a new house in Flint and a house up north for the wedding."

Jack had given her a price range and told her to go for it while he worked on the rest of things. Taking the job would mean being moved by the end of the month in order for Jack to start his new job on the 3rd of November.

Mother Kasey walked downstairs and kissed her baby girl on her forehead. She was glad to see her up and eating. It meant her strength and appetite was coming back. She wasn't aware of the nice little boost of energy she had gotten from Jack the night before.

"What are you up to this early?"

"Quite a bit actually, come sit down I have some news," Ivy said with a big grin on her face.

"Oh Lord, what have you come up with now girl?" Her mother knew that look in her daughters face. She just prayed it wasn't too over-the-top. Ivy was known for big ideas that seem almost impossible to achieve, but this one, however, had come from Jack.

She shared with her mother all the events of the last evening and how Jack's new job would have them moving into Flint and that they had set a wedding date. That, of course, was great news because now Ivy and her mom would be closer to each other. Mother Kasey was also thrilled that her pregnant daughter would have the honor of being a married woman when the baby arrived.

"Okay, so when is the big day?"

"Well, it won't be big Mommy. Just a few of our close family and friends up north."

"Okay…When?"

"In three weeks…" Ivy said, hoping that her mom wouldn't have a fit. A shocked Mother Kasey just shook her head and laughed.

"You and Jackson are really made for each other. The ideas you two come up with never cease to amaze me."

"Well, I'm glad you're okay with this," Ivy said sighing in relief, "I've already found the perfect place and reserved it."

Ivy showed her mom the lake house she found near Lake Michigan. It was absolutely breathtaking and could comfortably house at least twenty people. Just perfect for the small intimate gathering they had in mind. Never would she have imagined finding a place like this that would still be available so late, but it was and she wouldn't take any chance of losing it. There was so much to be done now that the ball was rolling. The first thing would be the guest list. Hopefully everyone would be able to at least make the wedding day even if they couldn't stay at the lodge the entire weekend.

"So it seems like your mom wasn't at all surprised about how quickly things were moving," Dr. Gilbert said.

"Not at all," Ivy laughed. "If she knew one thing for sure, it was that Jack and I both were very impulsive in nature. We would get an idea and move on it so quick that before you know it's done and everybody just has to go with the flow. Ironically… it's one thing we have in common that drives us both crazy."

"I can believe that. Many times it's the things that two people have in common that frustrate them the most. That's why it's the opposites about us that make us compatible and not so much our similarities."

That made a lot of sense to Ivy. Often the things she admired most about Jack were the things that made him so much different from her. She smiled as she thought of some of those things and drifted off into never-never-land.

"You still with me Ivy?" Dr. Gilbert laughed.

"Oh yeah, I'm still here."

"Where'd you go just that quick?"

Ivy laughed.

"I started to think of all the things about Jack that I love so much and most of them are the complete opposite of me," she admitted.

"Interesting thought, huh? We spend so much time convinced that we need to find someone we have so much in common with that we forget that differences can be good and sometimes better."

"But, Julia, the problem is no one tells you that until you get here when it's so close to being too late."

"You know one of the things I love about my faith is that, with God, we know that all things are working together for our good. So as long as were breathing and we believe... there isn't a 'too late'. You have so much love you drift off into space just thinking about him. Trust me, you're far from 'too late'. Now, I've just, for the first time heard any excitement from you about wedding plans. I wouldn't take you as the kind of woman who could have a small wedding. It's interesting to me that it was your plan. Let's talk about that."

The older Ivy had gotten the less important it became to have a big wedding. She was much more concerned about being a great wife and mother than being a fabulous bride. Having spent so much of her life in front of audiences, having this kind of intimate wedding would be so much more meaningful. It is just what she wanted. It was almost nerve wrecking that finally, after so many of life's blows, Ivy's dreams of love were coming true.

"So was it really about wanting the intimacy?" Julia asked.

"That was only part of it. I mean by nature I'm an entertainer and used to putting on a great show, but I didn't want it to be about that."

"What did you want? Really, honestly and truly what kind of wedding did you want?"

She sat quietly and thought for a moment and tried intensely to hold back the tears. Ivy was hesitant to say out loud what she really desired.

"Ivy, why is it so hard for you to say what you want?"

Blotting her eyes she replied, "Because if I don't get it I'll have to live with the resentment of what

I allowed myself to believe was possible," she finally confessed. "I know it's complicated and backwards and totally against what I believe as a Christian, but I'm afraid. I feel even worse because I haven't trusted God enough to give me what I prayed for even when it's right in front of me," she cried.

"You can't beat yourself up for being human. We work diligently to grow in our spirit so it's stronger than the flesh. God is not angry with you because of your lack of trust. It comes from our human side. Our spirit knows nothing of God that isn't trustworthy so we have to look at our human experiences to find where the seeds of doubt and mistrust were planted."

"I know where it comes from," Ivy admitted. "My dad..."

"Okay. Why is it there?"

Ivy explained how, although the end of her parents' marriage was traumatic, it was even more painful when her father had remarried. She wasn't surprised so much that he had remarried more than the fact that he did so without his children. Sure they were adults, but he had started a brand new life that didn't include them and Ivy was devastated. One thing she made very clear was that she had no interest in meeting the woman. Unfortunately, her father's new wife made the dreadful mistake of forcing herself into Ivy's world and it went terribly wrong.

"My dad rarely called me," Ivy began to explain. "So, if I got more than one call from him in a day, I assumed something was wrong. This evening in particular he had called four times and I figured I needed to call him back."

"Why hadn't you answered?"

"I had company in the house. The band was in town for a rehearsal and they were all staying with me. I wasn't trying to ignore him."

"Oh, I see. You said he rarely called, do you know why that is?"

"I don't know. My guess would be that maybe it's because I'm a lot like my dad. I can be very cold when I'm dissatisfied and I think he hated to hear that in my voice. So he kind of just left me alone."

"Hmm. So when you called him back, what happened?"

When Ivy called back, her dad began asking her questions about her eldest sister Ivonne as if he was completely unaware of reality. Frightened, Ivy sat at the table and began to cry. She thought her father was losing his mind. Only to find out that she was on speaker phone and it was his wife that wanted the answers to all these questions because she didn't believe that her sister was really her sister. The woman actually had the arrogance get on the phone, angry, loud and rude in an attempt to have a conversation with Ivy about feeling disrespected because her husband had invited his daughter to come to his home without her consent.

Ivy couldn't believe her ears! In shock and disbelief, she listened for a moment to make sure she was hearing correctly and hadn't slipped in to the twilight zone. Once she got her mind around what was happening…Ivy snapped.

"I really did try to be calm," she explained to Julia. "I started talking just to stop that woman from saying another word, but before I knew it, I was frantic and screaming at the top of my lungs."

Ivy was going to make sure it was known that no one had been disrespected more than she had. Her father and this woman had gotten married and hadn't had the decency to tell his children until three months after it had happened.

"Your father called you three months after he'd been married and then told you?" Julia asked.

"No, he called my sisters and my brother and told them. He never told me. They did."

"Had they met her before this particular incident over the phone?"

"They all did. They had been married for almost a year by this time and I was the only one who had not talked to her or seen her."

"Why was that?"

"I didn't want to. I didn't then and I still do not trust her. In my opinion any woman who doesn't make it a priority to know a man's children before she becomes a part of his world is selfish. I hated that she was my father's choice, but even more so at that time that he would allow that stranger to talk to me the way she did. I knew then that I was no longer who I used to be with my dad."

"Which was what? You were still his daughter nothing will ever change that."

"No, Julia, I wasn't just his daughter. I was a diehard daddy's girl. You don't go from that to nothing and not feel some type of way. That's what happened. I was a girl who had grown up with a full-time, very involved and supportive dad and it was as if overnight I felt like I was fatherless. Not because of some tragedy or illness that took him away, but because he had chosen to stop being my father!"

"And that made you feel?"

"It made me realize that anybody, no matter how much they love you, can just walk away. If my father could choose to leave, there is nothing stopping any other man from just walking out of my life. It's never good when a girl doesn't have a father figure, but when you have a good one and then as an adult he decides that his duties are over, it drastically warps your faith in a man's ability to love you forever."

"I agree and we'll work through that," Julia promised. "So how did this fallout come to an end? Was there any resolve?"

It just so happen that Ivy's mother and sister Ivory were stopping by to pick up some things. When they got to Ivy, she was on her way outside to avoid making her guests anymore uncomfortable than they had to be. Hearing her sister completely lost in anger and pain, Ivory had snatched the phone from her hands and their mother grabbed her and held onto her baby as she cried intensely. That night Ivory told their father that he was no longer allowed to talk to Ivy unless he went through her. Every stunt he pulled left Ivy in a state of depression that played havoc on her body. Ivy would be sick for weeks and Ivory wasn't going to let it happen ever again.

Once things slightly calmed down and they got Ivonne on the phone they discovered that she, too, was in tears of anger. Earlier she had gotten a call from James' wife threatening her to never come near her father ever again. It was complete chaos, which the Kasey girls were not accustomed.

The Kasey girls were raised to be peaceful, God-fearing Christian ladies. They weren't classless "hood rats" that snatched off earrings, fought in the streets and used indelicate language to express their discontent. They weren't suckers either. The line had been drawn that night and if that woman ever tried to cross it again there would definitely be trouble.

"After that night," Ivy continued. "It was a little over a year before I talked to my father again. So to answer you earlier question, I've always wanted a big wedding with all my family and friends present, but I couldn't fathom the idea of walking down that aisle without my daddy. I just never thought he'd come without her and I didn't want to be the bad guy for making him choose."

Chapter 12

Now back in session with Jack, Dr. Gilbert asked, "When, exactly, were you planning to tell Ivy that your new boss was her father?"

Jack knew that eventually he would have to tell Ivy the truth about his new job, in that it involved her estranged father, but he wasn't completely sure how it would go over.

"I was going to do it as soon as possible. I didn't want to drag it out. I had some business to finish up and the police station first though."

Back at the station, Jack was saying his goodbyes to his old friends at the Rochester Police Department. All they knew was that he was being transferred into Flint on a new assignment. Although they would miss him, they were all happy for him. Sully, his partner, of course was the saddest to see him go. He was proud of what this young man had accomplished with his time there and that he had been along for the ride. It wouldn't be easy for the two to say goodbye.

With his desk packed up he headed down to the garage with Sully at his side. It was a quiet walk. They had been like father and son on the job. The wisdom of Jack's older, salt and pepper haired, Italian partner had saved his life many times over the years. He knew moving forward he would still need that guidance.

"Sully, I can't give you all the details of this new assignment yet, but I can tell you that I'm still gonna need you."

"Kid, I got two more years before I can retire with a solid severance; I'm not going anywhere."
They laughed.

Jack set his box inside his truck and then gave his old partner a firm handshake. Sully pulled his young rookie in for a big hug.

"Keep your eyes open kid…this ain't over," Sully said, responding the way he had always did.

That had been his way of letting Jack know that there was always more news to come and that they needed to be ready for anything. Jack got inside his truck and with Sully's two pats on the hood, for the last time, he drove off the grounds of the Rochester Police Department.

"So, then you went home to talk to Ivy?" Julia asked.

"No, I went to my parents' house to pick up my daughter and talk to them about the wedding plans and the new job."

Without delay, Jack drove straight over to his parents' house where Mother Benett was preparing her grand-daughter to go back home with her father. Being only two- years-old and having no idea what had happened to her mother, Melanie was adjusting rather well. Of course, she had her crying fits in which she would call out for her mommy, but they could all understand that. The only solution was to love her through it. The best part was that she had a great daddy that she simply adored. He made everything better.

All four of his brothers were meeting him their mother's house, not knowing they were about to be invited to a wedding. They all had their own lives, but he was praying they would all be with him on his big day. Besides his twin, Jordan, his other brothers were still bachelors, well known and very eligible bachelors at that.

The Benett boys were known for being five of the most handsome men a woman would ever lay her eyes on. Now that both of the twins were spoken for, that left Jasper, Jason, and Jupiter who would be more than happy to get to a wedding and locate the single women. Unfortunately it wouldn't be the big shindig they had always thought their brother would have, so the hunt would have to wait.

The second Jack walked in the house he could hear Mel running towards the front door to see if it was her daddy. When she saw him she just fell to the floor and started laughing waiting for him to pick her up and tickle her. He did just that. Her incessant and adorable laughs brought everyone into the front room to greet him.

"Well, look who's here! Ain't you the black guy from Miami vice?" said Jack's eldest brother Jupiter who really thought he was funny.

They all laughed.

As Jack held his daughter in his arms he began to share with his family the good news with his job.

Waiting until they were all wrapped up in being very proud of him, he then decided to share with them the next bit of information.

"I'm glad you all are so happy, so you won't mind joining me and Ivy for our wedding…in three weeks," he said smiling and nodding. Everyone paused and looked at him like they had seen a ghost. They were in shock. Jack just laughed.

"Jackie, did you say you're getting married in three weeks?" Mother Benett asked.

"Yes, ma'am."

"I mean, I think Ivy's a great girl, but why such short notice? I thought you all were going to wait until after the baby is born?"

"We were Mom, but with this new job I have to move to Flint and you know I'm not leaving her in Rochester and I don't want to be apart from her while she's pregnant. I'm trying to do right by her. Would you rather us just shack it up?" he teased.

"Hush boy," his mother laughed.

"Besides, it's nothing big, just our immediate family and closest friends at a nice lodge up north.

After the baby is born we're going to have a big reception back home. So you guys are coming right?"

"Of course, we are, baby boy," Jupiter confirmed, speaking for the whole family as usual. Jack was the youngest of the five Benett boys and they would all, without question, be in attendance for his big day. Confident that he would have his family at his side, Jack returned home with his daughter to check in on Ivy and her side of the plans.

"So, then I went home to talk to Ivy about the job." Jack explained to Dr. Gilbert.

"How did that go?" she asked, listening intently.

Jack and Ivy sat on the couch in the living room working out the details of the weekend to come. Happy to have a new grandbaby, Mother Kasey took Mel into the extra bedroom and put her to bed. They began with the guest list and the numbers were already adding up. With Jack's four brothers, sister-in-law, parents, Sully and his wife, his side of the guest list was at nine. When Ivy added her side of the list they were over the maximum capacity of the house. After including herself and Jack, with his daughter and her god-son, they were at twenty-one. Her two sisters would, of course, be in attendance along with her brother, his wife, and their daughter. All that was left was her mom, Kayla and Tank.

"You can take Sully off the list for the house. He and his wife won't stay the whole weekend. They're just driving in for the day."

"Okay, so that takes us down to nineteen." Ivy said relieved.

"What about your dad?"

"What about him?"

"Sugar…"

"Jack, I don't have a problem with my dad coming, but *she* is not invited. If he can come without her then fine, but good luck with that."

"What if I told you that I already invited him? And that I made sure he knows she can't come."

Ivy laughed.

"Yeah, right. You don't even know my father."

When Jack didn't laugh she took another look at his face. He was serious. She sat up straight and looked Jack directly in his eyes.

"When did you talk to my father? And why?" Ivy quickly demanded to know.

"When I went to D.C., he's the reason I was called out there. Your father is my new boss sugar.... He's the one that offered me this job," Jack confessed.

"What?" Shouted a very shocked Ivy.

She didn't even know that her father still worked in government. That's how out of touch they had been. Now he would be the man in charge of her husband's career. Ivy didn't know if that was supposed to be a good thing or a bad thing.

As Jack told her the whole story, she sat there with her arms folded and had moved slightly away from him on the sofa. Ivy was upset that he hadn't told her everything to begin with, but of course Jack knew how to deal with his lady. He grabbed her by her waist and with one quick pull, moved her back over to him. There was no squirming for Ivy once Jack Benett had her in his arms.

"Quit trying to be mad girl. It's okay."

"I am mad," she said leaning her head back on his shoulder. "You should have told me this before."

"I'm telling you now. You trust me, don't you?"

"Of course, I do."

"Then you have to trust that I'm doing the right thing for us."

Jack included the details of his very candid conversation with Mr. Kasey concerning this job and his daughter. Ivy wasn't buying it. Nobody said just anything to her dad. He was a very intimidating man, which is why none of her boyfriend's ever got close enough to meet him. When Jack told her what he said to her father, she looked at him like he was crazy.

"Jack there is no way you talked to my dad that way. What really happened? Is he making you take this job to keep an eye on me?"

"He's not making me do anything, but, yes, he does want to keep an eye you. You are his youngest daughter and you were almost killed because of me. If I was in his shoes I'd probably be doing the same thing to make sure my daughter would be safe and well looked after."

"You're serious?"

"Yes!"

"So … is he coming?"

"He gave me his word and his blessing."

"His blessing?"

"Yes. Like a gentleman, I asked your father for your hand in marriage."

Ivy just shook her head. This man always had something up his sleeve and lately all of it was making her smile.

"I mean, I already knocked you up, what was he gonna say?" Jack joked.

"Shut up!" She laughed.

"How's your body feeling?"

"Pretty good. It's really not as bad as it looks. The hardest things are trying to lean forward or backward too much, but the stretching everyday helps."

"That's good to hear. You make sure and get your rest and keep stretching. Come October 29th we will be banging it out."

Ivy laughed out loud.

"Will you shut up? Mommy is right in the other room with Mel."

"Sugar did you forget you were pregnant? You think your momma don't know we get it in?" Jack teased. "Besides she can't hear me."

"Yes I can!" Mother Kasey yelled from the bedroom. "Cool your jets in there," she teased

"Yes, Mother!" they both laughed as they cuddled up like two devious teenagers.

Jack admitted to Dr. Gilbert that Ivy took the news much better than he had anticipated.

"What did you think she would do?" Julia asked.

"I knew she'd be upset I wasn't expecting her to give in so quickly, but I wasn't complaining."

"So at that point everything seemed to be looking pretty good. The wedding plans were moving forward and everything was on the table concerning the new job."

"Right. At that moment everything seemed to be almost perfect."

"So what happened?"

Jack stood up and looked out of the 21st floor window of Dr. Gilbert's office. Staring out at the cloudy skyline of the city he solemnly replied, "Some other dude happened." He turned and looked right at Julia and said, "She got involved with some other dude."

Chapter 13

The pale-faced Dr. Gilbert sat with one eyebrow wrinkled in as she was processing what she just heard. Had Jack just stated that the woman he loved, who was pregnant with his child, cheated on him? If that was indeed what he had stated, Julia was going to do her best to remain neutral and let the story unfold.

"You're saying that Ivy physically got involved with another man?"

"I don't know the details, and frankly, I don't want to."

"Jack you're making a very serious accusation against her, it would be foolish not to know the truth."

"The truth could make me hurt somebody and I love my job too much to go to jail," Jack stated honestly as he sat back down in the chair. He knew if he had all the details of this alleged affair it could be a catastrophe.

"Okay, so if you're unwilling to learn the entire truth, can you at least share with me what you do know?"

"Fine," Jack took a deep breath and began to recount the first moment he knew something was up. "So I accidently came across a few emails sent back and forth between her and some guy named 'Mark'."

"How was this an accident?

"I often just jump on her computer if it's closest to check emails or something and once I got on I realized that I was in her email. She was already logged in and she had a message from him and I read it."

"Why'd you read it?"

"I don't know."

"Before we get into what the emails said, let me ask you, were you already suspicious of her?"

"A little bit."

"Why? Did it have anything to do with that comment Curtis had made about him not being that man that you should be worried about?"

"I actually had kind of forgotten about that comment until she had started being so quiet."

"What do you mean? Quiet in what way?"

"Like she had gotten almost robotic you know? She just did what she did like it's what she knew to do, but there was no energy. She was cold and distant and…she wasn't laughing anymore."

"When did this behavior start?"

Jack scratched his head as he tried to think back to when Ivy had started to shut down. It had been nearly six months now and he couldn't pin point every moment that had happened since.

"I think it was about a week before the wedding. I remember her asking me if I sure that this is what I wanted and I said, absolutely! Then, she asked if I would understand if she wanted to postpone the wedding just until she was settled at home and I was settled on the job. I said ok."

"Was it really ok with you to postpone the wedding?"

"No."

"Then why did you agree?"

"I could tell she was a bit overwhelmed and I didn't want to rush her so I just said ok."

"It just seems like everything had been moving so smoothly. Was there anything that you can think of that made her question if this is what you wanted?"

Was there anything in the days just before you had this conversation?

"All we were doing was preparing to move. I had decided to start the job a week early to get a head start on team building so we could meet our first deadline with no trouble. She said she was ok with it, so that Wednesday, before I had gone into the office, I made sure she had help at the house. I had covered all my bases."

Even in that moment Jack was replaying that week in his mind and he couldn't find a moment when he had missed a beat. But for whatever reason that was the week Ivy had postponed the wedding and from that day forward things begin to slowly go downhill. He just hadn't noticed it right away.

"The only thing I can think of was maybe she was upset that my brothers and I hadn't gotten our suits when I said we would, but that's nothing."

"Are you sure it was nothing?"

"I mean it's not like I would have a wedding without a suit so I can't imagine why she would trip."

"Unfortunately, Jack, it doesn't take much for a pregnant woman to 'trip' as you say. But what was the reason behind you not getting the suits?"

"I was with my brothers and we hadn't all been together in such a long time. We really spent most of the day eating and catching up."

Great Lakes Crossing in Auburn Hills is way too attractive with gadget-filled stores and designer watches for the Benett Boys to stay focused on clothes alone. It had also been quite a while since they were all together this way and they were more in the mood to just have the opportunity to sit around and just be brothers. So a table a Bar Louie captivated their attentions for the better part of the afternoon.

They were really interested to learn more about this girl of whom it seemed their baby brother couldn't live without. After the number Lisa had done on his heart they were sure another committed relationship for Jack would be light years away. Jack had time to share with his twin the real story of what happened with Lisa, but the other three had not known the truth. Now seemed as good as time as any. It would be the only way they would understand the depth of his love for her.

By the time Jack got to the meat of the story revealing the mother of his firstborn to be a murderous mobster, his brothers were literally on the edge of their seats in disbelief. They had all met Lisa and patted their baby brother on the back for doing so well for himself. There was no doubt that Lisa was physically gorgeous, but they had no idea such beauty could be capable of such evil. His brothers did prove one thing. That, even after all the years of history that offers the wisdom of not judging a book by its cover, a man can still be blinded by superficial beauty. Thus, explaining why the three eldest brothers were still bachelors.

"So this was really some high crime drama you were wrapped up in?" Jupiter questioned.

"Yeah, life got extremely real! And that's why I was keeping my distance. After they kidnapped Nephew I couldn't risk anybody else getting hurt."

"You know the family never blamed you for that though right? Let's make that clear," Jasper quickly stated.

They had said repeatedly over the years to Jack that none of them blamed him for that incident. Jack blamed himself regardless and wouldn't be satisfied until his nephew was returned. Once he did that he felt comfortable again to sit at the table with his brothers. These four men had accomplished so much and their common goal was to make their parents proud. Jack never wanted to be the weak link that couldn't live up to the great standard of the Benett men.

Jason, still intrigued by the story wanted Jack to finish. So he did. He completed the tale that he wished was only a dream as his brothers sat wide-eyed and in shock that this had been his reality. In the past when something happened to one brother it happened to them all and together they dealt with it.

Since Jack went to the navy that fellowship wasn't as sound. The issues he dealt with as an officer couldn't be solved by telling his brothers so they could go and fight with him or on his behalf. Things had to be done by the book. A book that had rules that his brothers were not bound by as he was. They felt some kind of way about not being able to "brother" their brother during such a difficult time. However, they would be sure to never let him push them away like that again.

"I just want to be sure of one thing," Jasper said, "Tell me you're not marrying this girl just because you feel guilty for what happened on that island."

They were all thinking it, but no one was going to say it, but Jasper. Although she sounded like a great girl, they knew it would not be a good situation for him to marry out of guilt. Jack quickly set the record straight.

"I bought her that engagement ring eight months before this had all happened. I knew she was the one when I first met her. Things just seemed like they're moving fast now because I have this new job and we have to move, but I just wanted things to be done right."

It was very much the truth. It was also the truth that Jack knew he had not proven to do well about balancing his work and personal life well and wanted to use this time in between jobs to practice some better habits.

Dr. Gilbert swiftly interjected, "And how were you doing practicing that balancing act now that you had started the new job? And earlier than you originally planned?"

"I thought I was doing it well," Jack responded quickly.

About two months had passed since the postponing of the wedding and Jack was still assuming that everything was fine. Ivy had moved out of her apartment and into her mother's house, she was back to writing and adjusting well to being a mother to Jack's daughter. He was working and loving the new challenges of his job, but even more so that it got him home by 6 p.m. every night. For the most part, he no longer worked super late nights or weekends and was finding it much more freeing to enjoy his family. It was around the beginning of the third month that he started to realize that, although he was spending less time at work, it hadn't equated to more time with Ivy. In fact he was seeing her a lot less and she still hadn't set a new date for the wedding.

"She said that once Kayla's wedding was over then it would be easier to work on ours. So then it was a month after and we still had no date."

"How was it you were seeing less of each other?"

"Well she spent her days with Mel, and was still doing a lot of writing at night before she went to bed. So most days when I would come pick up Mel after work she'd be tired and just want to sleep. I understood but I didn't like that we weren't in the same house, which was why I was ready to get married so at least she'd be home and I could be with her." As it was, her mother was assuming all the care for Ivy that Jack felt belonged to him.

"What were your weekends like?"

"We were together on the weekends mostly. We would do something fun with Mel or we would just stay in and relax."

"Did you talk about the wedding at all?"

"Not much. Any time I brought it up she would change the subject. So I stopped bringing it up. I wasn't about to keep asking her. And I was already starting to feel like she just didn't want to get married."

Julia was a bit puzzled. She couldn't put these two scenarios together with the same people. Whatever Ivy had to say about her behavior was definitely the missing link. She closed her booklet and took off her big round glasses and rubbed her tired eyes.

"Okay, Jack, well, I think that's our time for today. We will continue on Thursday." This had been their third individual session and Julia was now believing they would start that joint session a lot sooner than she thought. "Did you have plans to see Ivy at all this weekend?"

"Yeah, we're supposed to go shopping for the baby's room on Saturday."

"How have things been since you all started therapy?"

"Awkward," Jack admitted.

"Well, we'll get rid of that here soon," she said confidently.

Jack stood from his chair and shook her hand. He didn't know why, but he believed her. Maybe it was his last strand of hope, but he believed that once all this was over, and Ivy got a chance to say whatever it was she needed to say, he would finally get to peace. In Jacks mind, peace was coming home every night to his Sugar.

Before he walked out of the office, Jack pulled an envelope out of his pocket and handed it to Dr. Gilbert.

"What's this?" she asked.

"These are the emails I read. Thought you may want to take a look."

He calmly walked out and shut the door quietly behind him.

Chapter 14

Monday afternoon had arrived quicker than Ivy had hoped. She was on the elevator on her way to see Dr. Gilbert for her fourth session and she was getting restless. Although it was good to be able to vent some of her frustrations she knew that if Jack wasn't hearing it all, then it wouldn't make things any better. After their very quiet shopping trip on Saturday she knew these joint sessions would need to get started very soon. She missed him, but wasn't convinced that just saying that would clear up months of disappointment.

Ivy stood still as the heavy elevator continued to rise towards the 21st floor. She was alone and the sound of rails and rings of the passing of floors was all she could hear. The kicking baby inside didn't too much like the ride so she wrapped her arms around her round belly to calm him or her. Ivy quickly walked off as soon as the doors opened and was hoping Julia was ready to see her, and, she was. Before Ivy could sign in, Julia's assistant was coming to get her and bring her inside.

The huge window in Dr. Gilbert's office was drinking in a massive amount of sunlight this afternoon. So, as an already glowing Ivy walked in, the sun intensified her radiance.

"I must say, Ms. Ivy, you wear the pregnancy very well! You are just beautiful today!" Julia exclaimed.

Ivy smiled and thanked her as she made herself comfortable on the couch. In the warmer months Ivy always switched her hair color to a lighter brown versus the jet black she wore during the winter. Now it was March and her hair mirrored the color of her big brown eyes that also got lighter in the spring.

Ivy looked like sweet caramel from head to toe that was so wonderfully complimented by the grey and burgundy caftan that covered her body. It was nice of Julia to compliment her, but these days Ivy always dressed as if any moment Jack would walk into the room. She loved the look on his face when he saw her at her best and she hadn't seen that look in a while. Most days when Jack saw her he was trying his best not look directly at her.

"So when we left off you were sharing why you hadn't planned on having a big wedding and the concerns with your father coming to give you away."

"Right."

"Okay, so now you've learned the truth about Jack's job and that your father has accepted his invitation. How were you feeling about the wedding plans then?"

"I was little nervous, but I was happy. Although I wasn't going to be totally convinced until I actually saw my dad there, but before I knew it there was no wedding to see him at. I had asked Jack if we could postpone it."

"Why? I know you were becoming overwhelmed, but was that really the reason?"

"I was overwhelmed, but, no, that wasn't the only reason," Ivy sighed. "Jack had decided to go back to work a week early and at the time I thought it would be okay because we were getting so much support from our families."

"But, it wasn't ok?"

"No. As soon as he said he wanted to go back early I knew we would right back to where we were before with no boundaries between work and family. I felt like nothing had changed. And I started to shut down."

"So why didn't you say that?"

"I didn't think it would matter! If he wanted to go back early, he clearly didn't see how important it was for him to be at home and I didn't want to stop him from being where he wanted to be," Ivy said with a great deal of attitude.

"But, Ivy, he will never be able to read your mind. You keep making this about a choice he has to make between you and his job and I don't think you're giving him enough credit. What had he done to make you feel so quickly that nothing had changed?"

"I had agreed to him going back to work on one condition."

"Which was?"

"Jack was good for not answering his phone and most of the time it was because he was so preoccupied with his job. With everything that had happened, and me being pregnant, it just didn't sit well with me that I would have to go back to that level of insecurity. So as long as he promised to be at every doctor's appointment and that I could count on him to be available should there be any emergency, I agreed."

"That sounds fair enough, but I'm guessing that didn't happen?"

"The first week he went back to work we had an appointment with the OB/GYN and he didn't show up."

"Why didn't he show up?"

"I still can't tell you because he still hasn't realized he missed it."

"You never said anything?"

"No ma'am. After that first missed appointment I didn't say a word. When he came to pick up Mel that day he was so excited about his day at work I never even brought it up. So from then on I would have my mom or Kayla go with me to the doctor."

"When Jack didn't show up that day what exactly did you feel?"

Ivy shook her head as she tried to put into words what that day was like.

"I don't know if it was just me being hormonal or what, but I felt stupid. Stupid for believing that just because I was having a baby, I'd magically move up on his priority list. Not to mention I had agreed to give up so much for us and to see that he wasn't doing the same really pissed me off."

"You realize though that some of what you gave up was for your own health right? With or without Jack in the picture you still didn't need to be traveling and working as hard. I just don't understand why you wouldn't ask him why he missed the appointment. Why let this sit in you for months and allow him the space to keep disappointing?"

"Jack doesn't listen. I guess I wanted him to finally figure something out for himself. I didn't want to be nagging or mothering him, telling him what to do all the time. I figured, 'my God we're both adults!' This time it wasn't about my stuff that he was missing, but this concerned both of us and it still wasn't enough for him to be there!"

Ivy was clearly upset at this point.

"So what did you do?"

"I asked him flat out was he sure this is what he wanted."

"What did he say?"

"He said, absolutely, this was what he wanted."

"But you didn't believe him?"

"No."

"So you postponed the wedding."

"Yes."

"What were you hoping would happen?"

She sighed. "I was hoping that having more time would give us both more of an opportunity to balance everything. I was hoping that maybe he would realize something was missing and come after it."

"And when he didn't?"

"Well, Julia, that's how we ended up here."

Dr. Gilbert sat back in her chair and thought quietly as she tried to decide what the next step would be. She now knew what set Ivy on a course to being robotic in her behaviors, but there was still more that needed to be acknowledged.

"This had to be building up quite a bit of tension and frustration. Was there anything you were doing to relieve that?"

"As a matter of fact there was. I had started going back to the gun range with my cousin at least once a week."

"The gun range?" Dr. Gilbert said looking up from her pad.

"Yes ma'am."

"Wasn't that kind of dangerous?"

"My doctor had cleared me to go as long as I didn't go alone. Kayla had the same concerns when we first went." Ivy went on to share with Julia the details of their first trip to the range after the incident. Kayla was very concerned.

"You sure it's okay for you to be out here?" Kayla asked. She was used to Ivy coming out to the range to relieve stress, but her condition was quite different now.

"I'm sure. Trust me I'm always careful and Dr. Simon says it's okay."

"What did Jack say?"

"Nothing..." she hesitated, "I didn't tell him."

"That's because you know he wouldn't want you out here. Look, why don't we just go to the spa or something?"

"No!" Ivy snapped. "I'm sorry Kayla, but you have to understand..." she paused as they got to the other side of the door and walked into the range. "I never in my life felt so physically helpless until I had Lisa and her brother kicking the crap out of me and dragging me out of that hotel room!"

"Ivy…" Kayla tried to interrupt.

"I won't ever be so ill equipped, unarmed, or unable to protect myself! My personal space was invaded and I was helpless! That won't ever happen again!" Ivy declared with intensity.

"Fine. I'm with you. We need to be ready to protect ourselves."

Kayla simply agreed with her even though she worried. She knew Ivy was in no mood to hear a speech and the truth was there was nothing she could say. Although Kayla was fully aware that anything could happen whether you're prepared or not, nobody was there when Ivy was in that nightmare so she could understand her intense desire to keep herself protected. Kayla just went with her and supported her without any more questions.

Ivy walked into the range, put on her protective goggles and gloves and pulled her hair back into a ponytail.

"Are you coming?" she asked Kayla without even slightly turning her head.

"Yeah… I'm right behind you".

With the look of intensity, she walked toward her station. The carpet beneath her felt stiffer with every step and the closer she got to her assigned position, the less she heard the sounds of shots ringing around her. Once Ivy was standing directly in front of her target, she put in her ear plugs, then lifted her 9mm into position. She put her head down, took a deep breath and closed her eyes. All at once pictures of the island, the hotel room and Lisa began to flash inside her head. Attempting to shake it off, Ivy lifted her head and with eyes focused, she emptied her clip.

They had been to the gun range many times together over the years so it was easy for Kayla to notice the difference in Ivy's shot. In the past they would laugh at each other's targets due to how hilariously off they were, but Ivy wasn't cracking a smile and her shot was dang near perfect. If this is what it would take for her cousin to release those frustrations, then Kayla would stick by her. But her prayers for Ivy would change after today. Ivy needed complete healing physically and emotionally from the memory of Cuba.

After about forty-five minutes of shooting, Ivy agreed to leave. Her side began to ache and it was past time for her to take her medicine. She knew she was pushing it a great deal to be out at all, let alone at the range. Remembering her priorities and promise to Jack and her sisters, she let Kayla take her home.

They joked all the way home, but once inside and Ivy having her medicine, Kayla finally decided to come clean about her worries. Ivy sat in her chair and cuddled up in her quilt leaning back ready for the meds to start their work.

"So.... are you okay?" Kayla asked suspiciously

"What do you mean?"

"Ivy your shot in there was the closest thing to perfect I've ever seen. When do you get that good?"

"I've always been a lot better then you. I just didn't flaunt it because we were just having fun. Come on you shouldn't be surprised. My dad's in law enforcement and so is Jack. They both taught me a few things."

"I just want you to be careful. I know you're angry, whether you want to admit it or not, and, rightfully so. The look in your eyes was kinda scary."

Ivy laughed.

"Kayla, listen, I will be fine. I will also be prepared."

"Prepared for what though? It's over right? Lisa is dead, you're safe and no one is coming after you anymore."

"How do you know that?" Ivy snapped. "Lisa proved one thing and that's the fact that we don't know half of what we think we know about anybody! Nothing will ever be the same Kayla! Nothing!" She exclaimed loudly. Ivy paused and took a very deep breath. "I have a family now with the man I love. I finally have everything I've ever wanted and I will do whatever it takes to protect it. Naiveté is a luxury I can no longer afford!"

With tears in her eyes, Ivy didn't realize she was yelling. Kayla grabbed her near hysterical cousin, held onto her and just let her cry. For the first time since the incident Ivy let it all out. Finally, she admitted just how traumatic the whole thing had really been. She had been trying her best to be strong so the family wouldn't worry, but in that moment every honest fear rose to the surface and she could no longer hide. In her heart, Ivy wished Lisa was still alive so that they could face each other, but her being dead was only haunting her rather than giving her peace.

"Ivy you need to talk to Jack about this."

"No. I can't right now. He's excited about this new job, the baby, and we have the wedding to plan. Besides in his mind it's over…and…"

"If it's not over for you, it can't be over for him. You've got too much on your plate to keep all this emotion locked up. It's dangerously unhealthy."

"You know that Kayla was right," Dr. Gilbert said seriously. "It had only been a few weeks that you were released from the hospital with strict instructions to take it easy and, here you were, going to the gun range and trying to plan an impromptu wedding all while recovering and trying to grow a healthy baby. What were you trying to prove?"

In most other situations Ivy was always trying to prove to herself that she was indeed strong enough to do more than what the doctors told her. She hated limits and boundaries and wanted to be as free as everyone else to give all of herself into her work to get the greatest result, but her body wouldn't always let her.

Her medical conditions would rob her of that freedom and she fought it tooth and nail. She thought it made her inferior and incapable. Ivy felt crippled by the limitations and didn't take to the reality that she had a handicap. One that could simply be controlled by pacing herself and resting when she needed and sometimes just saying "no" to one or more people and projects. This time it wasn't about trying to keep up or prove she was strong enough to be great. It was about proving that she was strong enough to survive.

It was too much, however, Ivy was very conscious of the reality that everything can change in a second. With the unexpected chance of death still fresh in her psyche, she was unconsciously attempting to grab everything in life there was to live in only a few moments in order to beat the promise that tomorrow may not come. Something would have to give, but what?

"I was trying to live," Ivy said, "I didn't want to be cooped up in the house just wasting away in fear. I wanted to be prepared for anything."

"There was and still seems to be a lot of fear, which is understandable, but what is it exactly that you're afraid of?"

Ivy sat quietly for a moment hesitant to say what she really felt.

"I know it sounds crazy, Julia, but I am not confident that Lisa is dead."

Chapter 15

Just moments before it was time for Jack to come in for his appointment, Dr. Gilbert finally took a moment to read the emails that he had left in her hand. These few papers were the basis on which he had built his case against Ivy and so there had to be something extremely significant on these pages.

Google Chats
January 29
5:29pm

Ivy Kasey: Well look who it is!
Mark Delcoy: lol I was hoping you hit me
I been looking for you
Ivy Kasey: Really?
Mark Delcoy: For the last year... and then today I was looking for an old video you showed me
And then all of this stuff comes up
I thought if I left comments you'd get the message and respond. I couldn't get

	through all the videos. You know it still gets to me to hear you sing
Ivy Kasey:	lol yeah right.
	Why were you looking for me?
Mark Delcoy:	I plead the fifth...
Ivy Kasey:	bye
Mark Delcoy:	ok ok
	I missed u
	I admit it. Four years has passed and I still think about u and have spent the last year lookin for u
	Happy now?
Ivy Kasey:	Actually Delcoy… I am happy now
Mark Delcoy:	So you got a man now is what you're saying?
Ivy Kasey:	What I'm saying is I'm happy
Mark Delcoy:	well….
	That's all I ever wanted for u

January 30
8:07pm

Mark Delcoy:	Hey u
Ivy Kasey:	Hello

Mark Delcoy:	How are u?
Ivy Kasey	… happy
Mark Delcoy:	yeah yeah
Ivy Kasey:	What do you want Del
Mark Delcoy:	I want to talk to you
Ivy Kasey:	We are talking
Mark Delcoy:	You know what I mean
	Can I call you?
Ivy Kasey:	Ummm
Mark Delcoy:	really?
	I spent a year lookin for u…
	A year
Ivy Kasey:	Please shut up
	Ok
	We can talk

Dr. Gilbert turn both pages over, looking and hoping that there was more Jack was basing Ivy's unfaithfulness on. There was nothing else. It wasn't much at all, but she could see why Jack would be concerned. If anything it was the perfect amount of evidence to cause and maintain suspicion. With pages in hand, Julia paged her secretary out front and instructed her to send Jack on back to her office.

He walked in and she could see what Ivy was talking about when she described Jack as having an unassuming presence. You couldn't help but to feel the energy he brought into a space.

"Mr. Benett, how are we today?"

"Did you read the emails, Doc?"

"Straight to the point huh?"

"Yes."

"Ok fine. Yes, I did read them. I want you to tell me what you believe these conversations to mean."

"I think he's the reason why she hasn't set a date."

"I think it's clear that whoever this 'Mark' is that he still had feelings for her, but there is nothing on here to suggest that she returned any of his feelings. Wouldn't you agree?"

"Then why talk to him? If there wasn't anything going on then what did they have to talk about?"

"Why not just ask her?"

"Would she tell the truth?"

"Why not? Had she given you a reason not to trust her? We both know you know more about this 'Mark' than you're saying. So what did you find out? Do you know him?"

Julia was nowhere near stupid and Jack knew it. They were both cops and had access to information most would never see and he had immediately found out everything he could.

Jack sat shaking his head. He finally sat back in the chair and told the good doctor what he'd found out.

"His name is Markus Benjamin Delcoy. He worked as a corrections officer in South Florida. He quit his job six months ago and moved back to Michigan. He's currently separated and has two children. And yes… I know him. We trained together at Annapolis. We went in to the SEAL program together, but Delcoy didn't make the cut."

He had just unloaded much more information that Julia even imagined. How many times was this story going to twist and tie together she wondered?

"Does Ivy know that you two know each other?"

"I doubt it. She knew him before she knew me. Why he's back here right now, that, I don't know, but I have been trying to find out." Jack admitted.

"Let me ask you this, Jack, do you think your lack of trust has anything to do with you not being trustworthy?"

"I've never been unfaithful!"

"Infidelity isn't the only issue that can cause mistrust. You said yourself you haven't been great at prioritizing your time. How was she to trust that when you weren't showing up for her it wasn't because you wanted to be anywhere but with her?"

"I know you're not going to make this my fault! You won't find any communication between me and another female that's inappropriate, but you have this proof right here that she's talking to another man!"

"Yes, but we don't know what these conversations consisted of. I'm not defending her, Jack, I'm trying to help you get to the reason why she would be doing what you're accusing her to be which is being unfaithful. With all this love between the two of you, why would she need anyone else?"

Jack had no answer.

"You said you haven't been unfaithful, but by your own admission, your work comes before her on a regular basis. True, you may not be with another woman, but being unfaithful means placing someone or something higher on your list of priorities than your relationship. Earlier you said and I quote, *the truth could make me hurt someone and I love my job too much to go to jail.* Do you love Ivy enough to not want to go to jail?"

"Of course, that's a given! It wasn't necessary for me to say that because she knows I don't want to be away from her."

"Does she? You keep repeating all the obvious things that you believe she should just know, but we're here Jackson because she does not know," Julia stated so passionately.

She wanted him to get it. To understand that without saying the words and applying the actions, there was no way Ivy would just know and keep believing that his love for her was real. If Ivy had been unfaithful, then she would have to come clean and admit her faults, but so would Jack. Julia was trying to help him understand that both persons in the relationship are responsible for making it work.

"Have you ever heard of the book called the '5 Love Languages'?"

"No, ma'am."

Julia got up and walked over to her desk and grabbed a copy of the book and handed it to Jack. She sat back down and looked at him over her big black round frames and said, "Jack, the best thing you can do for yourself in this next week is to read this book. I know that you two love each other, but if you're not speaking the same language then it's no wonder you're confused."

"Isn't next week our first session together?"

"Yes, and before it happens, you should know what's in this book. That will help us with the communication portion at least. Now there's one other thing we need to talk about alone before that session."

"What's that?"

Dr. Gilbert took a deep breath.

"Lisa."

"What about her?" Jack asked confused. How Lisa was any topic of discussion anymore wasn't making sense.

"Is Lisa over for you?"

"She's dead," he replied matter-of-factly.

"What's your point? We both know just because a person isn't alive doesn't mean that there still aren't unanswered questions, feelings of anger and whatever else that person left behind. What did she leave with you and is it affecting the way you love Ivy?"

He took a minute to think about it. Of course, she left things with him. Feelings of not just anger, but embarrassment. Jack prided himself on being a great officer and this woman had blinded him and drastically changed his life. He knew Ivy was nothing like her, but he couldn't help but question if loving her would eventually get him into the same kind trouble.

Love finally felt good to him, but it was almost too good. Ivy was almost too perfect. He had been waiting for her to be imperfect only to justify his lack of trust.

What he loved about his job was that he could expect a criminal to be just that - someone proven to be full of lies and deceit with intent to break the law for their own benefit. It shook his entire world to learn that the bad guy was the woman he was sleeping with. One that, to his knowledge, was completely on the up and up. Even with her gone, Lisa's betrayal was very much still with him. And, yes, Ivy was being punished for it, but so was he. Of course he didn't know how nor did he want to verbalize that. So he sat quietly.

"If you're suffering from Lisa's betrayal and making Ivy pay for it you're only going to push her into space where she can't win," Julia stated. "We will get to the truth about this guy, Mark, but if we find out that his intentions are to have her, the only way he can, is if you let him. So the question is Jackson, are you prepared to give her up?"

Chapter 16

Dr. Gilbert wasn't surprised by Ivy's confession. If anything it made more sense than anything else she had heard. The truth was that everything she was feeling about her relationship was only intensified because of the trauma concerning Lisa and she was the one person involved that they hadn't been discussing. A solemn Ivy was afraid to admit her fears because they made her feel outside of herself. After all she had gone through, the last thing she wanted to be called was "crazy".

"It's understandable that you have these uncomfortable feelings," Dr. Gilbert stated, hoping to comfort her. "You wouldn't be human if you didn't. What happened was very traumatic and it's not something that people get over quickly. That's why this kind of therapy is necessary."

"The hard part is that it was traumatic for Jack, too, but for him it's over. I feel so weak that I'm still bothered as much as I am, but he never talks about it."

"How do you know it's over for him? Has he said that?"

"No. But he won't talk about it."

"That could just be his way of moving forward, but it doesn't mean it's over for him. Just think, the whole time you were dating he never once brought up his missing nephew, but he was working on that case day and night. Just because he's not talking about it doesn't mean that it's over." Dr. Gilbert said, making a very valid point. "Like I said, it's normal to have fear that lingers after something like this. The key is not allowing it to take over your life. So, was this postponing of the wedding really about Jack missing the doctor's appointment?"

"It was because for me it was more than just a missed appointment. It was a reminder of what could happen if Jack doesn't show up and if he's not going to remember things and be conscious of where I am and...and that he should've been with me or ...or not answer the phone when I call and I get into trouble then I'd better know how to take of myself and our children." She paused and took a breath. "If I have him, but I still have to figure out how to live without him, then why are we getting married?"

It was finally out. The million dollar question.

Dr. Gilbert quietly took her notes and mentally began to process her thoughts. She understood where Ivy was and wanted to choose her words carefully.

"So tell me exactly why you're not confident that Lisa is out of the picture?"

"There was one other thing that started that week Jack went back to work…"

"What happened Ivy?"

"Night terrors," Ivy confessed.

Dr. Gilbert looked up quickly from her notes and directly into Ivy's mouth as if her words had dropped firecrackers into the pit of her stomach. She knew that night terrors meant that Ivy's emotional struggle with the trauma had become psychological which could mean more of problem then she anticipated.

"It started that night of the missed doctor's appointment and occurred about once every other week for the next two months. Then they increased."

"How often are you having them?"

"Once or twice a week…at least"

"And Jack doesn't know?"

"No."

"But he would if you got married and he saw it for himself."

"Right."

"But you admitted earlier that you had been foolish to doubt his love for you even through sickness, so why does the thought of him seeing you in terror scare you?"

"Physical illness is one thing Doctor, but mental illness is another and you know it."

Julia didn't want to alarm Ivy but she understood her concern and knew it was valid.

"Ivy, it's normal to experience these kinds of things."

"Julia, these terrors are just that! Terrifying! They are extremely vivid and feel so real..." she sobs. "I don't know how to stop it."

"Can you tell me what happens?"

Ivy took a deep breath and closed her eyes as she began to share with Julia this reoccurring nightmare that had been plaguing her.

"It always starts the same way...I'm on the beach praying when it gets very dark and a thunderstorm starts to crash into the island and then I'm back inside that hotel room."

With her eyes closed tight, Ivy explained how she slowly goes to the phone inside the room to call Jack and he doesn't answer. Then there's a knock at the door. She opens it but no one is there. She goes back to the phone and calls Jack again.

"Jack?"

"Come on Ivy… we both know Jack never answers his phone"

"Lisa?"

"*Muy bueno.*"

"What do you want?"

"Only to tell you *no hay finales felices*"

Lisa hangs up and Ivy stands still as bricks as the dial tone rings in her ear and with a crash of sudden thunder the power goes out. By the flashes of lightening blasting through the window, Ivy frantically searched for her cell phone when she heard the sound of something in the room moving slowly across the floor. Her heart began to pound in her ears as loud as the thunder. She knew she was not alone.

"Then, everything just goes black." Ivy says to Dr. Gilbert. "Then, all at once there are flashes of lightening and I'm falling back onto the glass table. In this dream I never lose consciousness and everything that happened moves so slow like scenes being played one at a time on an old movie reel. I can feel and see everything! The glass cutting into my head, Lisa kicking me, the wet sand and rocks scraping my legs and the cold water trying to pull me out to sea."

"Jack got to you before you slipped into the ocean right? In reality?"

"Yes, but not in the dream. I never see him. I'm drowning in the dream. When my mother wakes me up, she says that I'm desperately gasping for air or screaming and it's really difficult to wake me up. The worse things got with Jack the worse the nightmares have been. One night I stopped breathing altogether and if my mother wasn't there... we don't know what would have happened."

"What has your doctor said about this? I'm sure this must be dangerous for you and the baby."

"He insisted that I take advantage of the therapy because there's nothing medically he can do that wouldn't put the baby at risk. Dr. Gilbert, every night I go to bed I'm fearful of drowning in my sleep. I don't know how to tell Jack about this without him insisting that I be under constant medical watch and I don't want that!" Ivy said crying. "I know what the report says, but I feel like these dreams are trying to prepare me."

"Prepare you for what?"

"For the possibility that Lisa is alive and coming for her revenge."

Julia placed her hand on chin and took a deep breath. She had to ask Ivy flat out what she believed so she could properly help her deal with her truth.

"Ivy, even with the proof that Lisa was killed in that explosion, you believe that she is still alive?"

Without any hesitation, Ivy replied. "Yes, I do."

"And so you're preparing for what exactly?"

"Julia, I'm not crazy, but just as sure as I sit here before you if that woman ever again becomes a threat to me and my family I will be prepared to do what the FBI didn't." Ivy declared as her eyes got as cold as ice. "I will kill her."

Chapter 17

Dr. Gilbert sat in her office chair and faced the skyline outside her window. As she leaned back, she silently prayed for wisdom. She had unique cases before, but nothing quite like this. Although most of cases were with people who had experienced crime related trauma, she rarely met couples. The few she did see were so adamant about separating that the most she could help them do was provide peace of mind for the next level of decision making. Jack and Ivy were two people who were clearly in love with each other, but making it so hard to return to all the roads that got them there.

Today they would be inside her office together revealing things that they hadn't been able to get out for months. As she turned her small brown office chair back around to her desk, Julia took her gasses off her freckle-covered face and rubbed her eyes with her chubby little hand. All she could do was pray that they both had done the homework she had assigned.

Ivy was given the task to journal her next experience with the night terror and be prepared to come clean about why she shut down to begin with. Jack was supposed to have read the 5 Love Languages and be prepared to confront Ivy about this man, Mark. Only heaven knew what would become of this first meeting and with the sound of the phone buzzing indicating that a patient was present, heaven and earth were about to meet.

"Yes?" Dr. Gilbert replied to her receptionist.

"Mr. Benett is here."

"Thank you. Send him in please."

Jack walked in and looked around a bit trepidatious as he was unsure if Ivy was already there. He let out a sigh of relief and sat down when realized he was the first to arrive.

"Nervous?" Julia asked leaning back on the front her desk.

"Maybe a little," he answered honestly.

Not about seeing Ivy, but about the possibility that this meeting would not go well. He had heard all of what Dr. Gilbert had tried to explain about healthy arguing, but he didn't like it.

"No worries, Jack, everything will be fine. How was that book?"

"You know I'm not really into those kinds of books, but I think I understand the value in this one."

"Did you take the quiz online?"

"Yes ma'am."

"And what did you come up with? What was your love language?"

"Acts of Service," Ivy declared from the back of the room.

She had just walked in and stood at the door. Jack sat still for a moment. Her voice alone started his heart to racing. He finally stood up and turned around to greet her. He tried not to stare as she walked towards him, but he couldn't help it. She was beautiful.

The temperature had dropped a little from last week and so Ivy was dressed accordingly in a black, long sleeve, dress with a wide turtleneck. Her brown hair was resting on her shoulders alongside her blushing brown skin. Even more since pregnancy her breasts were large and proud and now they served as the top shelf above her big round baby-filled tummy. All of his favorite parts of her body were screaming out for him to touch. From her pout lips to her wide hips, everything was full just the way he liked it and the fact that it was all because she was growing his seed inside of her made him more attracted to her than she had ever been.

Ivy was trying her hardest not to look up into his eyes for fear that she'd just start crying, but she couldn't help it. He leaned down and kissed her gently on the cheek and he seemed taller than usual as she looked up and met those beautiful browns. It was a grey sweater that covered his broad shoulders and strong chest. It was her favorite color to see him in and Jack knew it.

He helped her onto the sofa and then took his seat at the other end. A perfect picture of the present wall of emotions that sat uncomfortably between them. Ivy could be as prim and proper as she knew how to be but the truth was that between her normal high sex drive, the hormones of pregnancy, and how much she missed Jack having his way with her, she was ready to burst.

"So is she right?" Julia asked breaking the tension.

"Right about what?" Jack asked. After looking at his love, he had lost all train of thought. "Oh! Oh yeah about the love languages. Yes, actually, she was right my highest score was Acts of Service."

"How did you know that Ivy?" Julia asked.

"I know Jack. His world can get very hectic so he notices and appreciates it when I get things done to make it easier for him," Ivy said smiling.

"Is that right Jack?"

"Yes ma'am," he grinned. "She is right."

"Do you think you know her love language?"

Before Jack could answer Ivy interrupted,

"Uh could we not do that?" She asked nervously, "I mean... can we get started?"

"Well, we have started Ivy. Is something wrong?"

Ivy sighed with irritation. She knew this road was a bad idea because there was no way Jack knew what her love language was, but she had committed to be open.

"No, ma'am, please continue."

"Thank you. So Jack, you want to take a guess about what Ivy's love language is?"

He sat back and thought for a minute. "I'm new to this idea of love languages, but I think hers is the same as mine, Acts of Service."

"Share with her why you believe that." Julia instructed.

"Well she..."

"Um, Jack..." Julia interrupted. "She, is right there. Tell her why you believe that."

Jack slowly turned to Ivy and without looking directly at her he continued.

"Well, I realize that you have a lot you do with your work, too, so I think you appreciate it when I get things done without you having to ask me. You know...like you do for me."

Ivy grinned a little.

"So Ivy is he right?"

"He's right in that I do appreciate it when he does things without me asking, but that's not my love language." Ivy said trying not to discourage him with her tone.

"So tell him what it is," Dr. Gilbert instructed.

"It's quality time."

There was an awkward silence.

"This is why I felt like starting here was a good idea. It's going to help you two be more open by realizing that part of the problem is that you're not speaking the same language," Dr. Gilbert spoke firmly, hoping they would feel confident in her plan. "Communication only works when we're speaking the same language. You can be talking as calm as you know how, but if Ivy is speaking Spanish and you Jack, are speaking Japanese, then what good will come of your conversation? What was your second highest score in the love language quiz?" she asked them both.

"Physical touch," they both responded in unison. They looked at each other and laughed a little. No wonder they had no disagreements in that area.

"See you have that in common, which is why you have such a strong physical connection which is great, but that can't hold up a relationship alone. You ever wonder why a relationship with great sex alone still won't last?" Dr. Gilbert asked. "Because sex doesn't require language, but relationship does, and since we're here to save a relationship we have start learning some new language."

It made the playing field as close to even as it had ever been. They were both made to understand from the beginning that they both had work to do. Jack was happy with that since his biggest fear of this therapy business was that everything would be made to be his fault somehow. But Dr. Gilbert had proved that she was neutral and trustworthy.

The doctor began to share with them some of her notes that she had taken from them both. Making it clear that before they started a dialog they both needed to be honest about how they got to where they were.

"Ivy, I want to start with you because it was your issue that has had the precipitating effect in events that have caused you to shut down."

Ivy took a deep breath and was hesitant to speak. She was so used to Jack cutting her off and not allowing her to finish her thoughts that she was almost choking on the words she had to say. This was her last hope of restoration and if he shut down on her it would break her heart.

"Remember, Ivy, you're here to talk to each other. This is a safe space."

"What's on your heart, Sugar?" Jack said calmly.

That's what he said to her when he was genuinely interested in what it was on her mind. When he knew she had been holding on to something.

Ivy just shook her head. Then, finally, she spoke.

"We made a deal before you went back to work and the first day you went back, you broke that deal."

"Be specific, Ivy. Remind him of the promise he made and help him to understand why it was so important to you," Julia urged.

"You promised that you would be at every doctor's appointment and that…"

"You haven't been telling me about them!" Jack interrupted.

"You're right, not since the very first one that I reminded you of for a week and you still missed!" Ivy snapped back. "No, I haven't said a word about them because, once again, your job was more important to you than me and I wasn't strong enough to fight for your attention!"

"So I miss one doctor's appointment and that was reason enough for you to replace me? Really?"

"What?" Ivy snapped, but before she could get into it any further Julia stopped them.

"Wait, Jack. Let's not jump into that." Julia instructed.

"No, let's jump into it because I want to know what he's talking about?" Ivy snapped.

"We need to deal with where we are now. Let's not make this a battle of infractions because we would all lose. One by one let's talk about the issues. Right now, what Ivy needs to know is why you missed the appointment, Jack. Do you remember?"

"Honestly, I forgot. Things were really hectic my first day in the office so it just slipped my mind, but it wasn't intentional. I don't know why you wouldn't just call me and remind me."

"Because I'm not your mother and I didn't want to be nagging you about when you were supposed to be somewhere. I thought maybe this time, since this pregnancy involved us both, and not just me, it would interest you enough to show up." Ivy replied.

"You think you and our baby aren't important to me? Really Ivy? I took a desk job with your father, of all people, as my boss for you and our family! That's not showing up? That doesn't tell you how important you are to me?"

This was the perfect example of the confusion of language that Dr. Gilbert had talked to them about. Jack was believing that his act of service in taking the job and working to provide for his family was equivalent to "showing up" for Ivy. When, in fact, she had been asking him to show up in the literal sense. She needed his presence to be where she was when she needed him. When he didn't come to the doctor's office that day all she understood was that the job was more important than she was because that's where he had chosen to be.

"Now let's pause and talk about what was just said. Ivy what did you just hear Jack say?"

Ivy sighed. She knew what he had said, but it irritated her. Now that she had a different perception did it mean that her past response was invalid?

"He said that his job is important because that's how he provides and takes care of us." Part of her wanted to stay with her reasoning so she could continue to be upset.

"That's exactly what I've been trying to say," Jack confirmed shrugging his shoulders like it was wasn't that hard to understand in the first place.

Ivy rolled her eyes as Julia asked them both to take a deep breath as they paused for a moment. She wanted to be sure to give them time to allow these truths to settle before they continued.

"Jack, do you know what character she refers to you as?" Dr. Gilbert asked.

He grinned.

"Um... yeah, she um..." he was a little embarrassed, "She calls me Batman."

"Do you know why?"

"That's her favorite comic book hero."

"Let me read to you what she said when we talked about it." Julia slipped her glasses on to the edge of her red nose and began to read from her notes.

"Jack loves his work. He's identified by the purpose in it and he's married to it. Although most people will never know just how much he does, every day he saves lives. But, I was almost a casualty of his dedication and

I feel like he feels that his love for me makes him weak. Weakness is something he can't afford when there are people's lives at stake. And, like Batman, he'll always find a way to save Gotham, the people, first, even at the risk of losing what he loves more. I'm afraid Jack will never let himself love me more than the need to save the world."

Dr. Gilbert removed her glasses and held then by her side with the notebook in hand. "Now, Jack, keep in mind what you now know in that Ivy is fluent in the language of quality time, and from that perspective, why does she call you Batman?"

He understood the reference in a different way now and he wasn't sure he liked it. He definitely didn't want to say it.

"Maybe because... because it was always hard for him to be both a hero and a regular guy."

"Your dedication and servanthood is admirable and understandable. You're a soldier and everything about your career requires your acts of service, but when you get home, what this woman needs is your time." Dr. Gilbert said.

"When I used to come home to her she had my time and my attention! Be honest," Jack said looking at Ivy, "When I first started working I was home every day before 6 p.m. right?"

"Yes, you were, but, Jack, you get the house, play with Mel for a while, start talking about your day and fall asleep. By the time you wake up you're going home to take Mel to bed and get ready for you next day of work and you don't always take her with you. You tell me what part of the day you actually spend with me?" Ivy asked.

"Well, it would be a lot different if I didn't have to make two stops to get home to be with you, but you're the one that called off the wedding," he snapped with an attitude.

Jack was going to make sure he put that bit of information out there just for clarity. In his mind they could be having plenty quality time if he was coming home and she was there and not at her mother's house.

"I postponed..." Ivy said. Then she paused and took a breath.

She was getting upset and she wanted to stand up to express her discontent. She grabbed the arm of the couch and struggled to try and pull herself up.

"What are you doing?"

"I'm trying to stand up," she snapped at Jack.

"For what?"

"Because I don't want to sit down!"

She was finally up on two feet and taking a deep breath as Jack was turning his head and sighing. Ivy was so determined to try and do more than she could handle and he wasn't going to fight with her.

"I postponed the wedding. I didn't call it off. There is a difference."

"Okay let's pause right here," Julia suggested. "One thing I believe is important is what Ivy meant when she said in that same statement, that you seem to *be identified by your work and that you're married to it*. Jack, you want to be married to her and it bothers you that she has not re-set your wedding date. Ivy tell him why you haven't done so."

And without hesitation Ivy bluntly said, "I feel like you're already married to that job and I don't want to be your mistress anymore."

Chapter 18

"If you don't want to be with me then what the hell are we even doing here?" Jack shouted.

Ivy shook her and turned towards the window. He hadn't heard what she said, but thank the good Lord that Julia did.

"Jack, Ivy didn't say she didn't want to be with you. What she said is that she wants to be number one with you. Do you understand?"

"No, I don't understand because she is number one! Nothing that I do for her, I do, or have ever done, for anyone else. It's all for her!"

"We just got though talking about our language and I know it's going to take some time, but you have to start trying to speak her language. You've made a great start by taking a job that hasn't been so intrusive to your personal life, but if you come home every day by six and you're still not spending that time, present in the moment with her than it's just like you're not there at all." Julia stated.

Jack wasn't understanding. To him, being home with her, even if he was sleeping, was still being with her.

"Is that how you were feeling Ivy?" Julia asked to clarify.

"Yes. I just wasn't getting what I needed."

"What do you need?" Jack asked frustrated.

Ivy turned and looked directly into his eyes. "Just you."

Dr. Gilbert knew Jack wasn't understanding and so she began sharing with them how people sometimes unnecessarily over compensate in areas that don't matter when the person who loves us only wants us. People package themselves inside so many pointless costumes creating false presentations of who they are only to find out that all a person wants is the genuine article. Our full and complete attention and the security of knowing that no one else can infiltrate that space. Just as Ivy needed it, so did Jack.

"Ivy, all you are really saying is that you need the confidence of knowing that you are enough reason for Jack to stay in this relationship. Is that right?

"Yes, ma'am, that's right."

"But, that same confidence you want, he should have to," Julia stated. Ivy looked back at Julia oddly wondering what she was trying to say.

"Jack, you had something you wanted to ask Ivy?"

She looked at him very suspiciously. Jack took a seat crossed his right leg widely over his left and sat back. Looking at Ivy like he was really about to pull the big gun out of the holster as he began to question her.

"Yes, I want you to tell me who 'Mark Delcoy' is and why you've been talking to him."

Ivy fought the urge to ask about why he even knew about Del because she knew it was a senseless question. Her man Jack was a detective and it didn't surprise her that he had been sniffing around and found something that he probably shouldn't have. The truth was, he had a right to know, and she wasn't going to hide.

"Mark Delcoy is a man I used to date about four years ago. About four or five months ago he contacted me out of the blue and said he wanted to talk. So we talked."

"About what?" Jack inquired.

"About life. He wanted to catch up."

"Catch up? Really? How did he even know how to find you? Did you tell him about Cuba?"

"Originally, he said he just wanted to catch up. And, no, I didn't tell him about Cuba… I didn't have to." She said turning again back towards the window and looking at the skyline. "He already knew about it."

Both Jack and Julia looked at Ivy very confused waiting for her to explain what she had just said, but she wasn't quick about it. Although her heart was racing, she stood there quietly watching the sun move slowly behind the city. She didn't think she was going to have to share this.

"What do you mean he already knew?" Jack demanded to know.

"From what I understand you couldn't even tell your families the truth until just recently and even that was limited. This guy could be dangerous." Dr. Gilbert added. It genuinely raised a concern for her because Ivy hadn't shared this information in their private session.

"He's not dangerous," Ivy assured them as she finally decided to turn and face them, walking over to the other chair to rest her legs, she confessed. "It was Curtis who told Mark about the accident and it was Curtis who told him how to find me."

As if Jack needed another reason to dislike Curtis, here was the last straw. Ivy went on to share with him and Julia the complete story of how and why Markus Delcoy came into the picture.

The week after Ivy decided to postpone the wedding, she had finally had the courage to tell Curtis she was leaving the band which also meant releasing him from his job as her manager. She knew it wasn't going to go smoothly and it would take Curtis some time to adjust, but the sooner she got it over with the better for them all.

Curtis was in town for a concert in Detroit that he had been hired as the musical director for so she and Kayla went to Detroit for the weekend and Curtis joined them for dinner Saturday night. The two of them sat in the corner booth at Beans & Cornbread and tried to work out a strategy before Curtis arrived.

"You realize that no matter how sweet you are about this, Curtis is not going to like it," Kayla said honestly.

"Yes I know, but the least I can do is make sure he knows it's not personal."

"But it is personal, Ivy. Everything about this is personal. If it was business then Curtis wouldn't be a problem, but you're leaving because of Jack and I don't like it either, but I understand. If you and Jack have any shot of making this work you need to eliminate as many unnecessary problems for yourselves as possible and Curtis being in love with you is a problem."

"No the problem is the fact that Curtis isn't in love with me. He's just petty, overprotective and doesn't trust Jack. We have enough problems on our own without Curtis in my ear reminding me of everything Jack does wrong."

That was really a problem because Curtis was really good at exploiting Jack's inability to be consistent and in his mind it was his job to protect Ivy. Curtis thought she was just too naïve and sensitive to see when something wasn't good for her and in the past he had been right. Several times.

They continued to discuss how the news of Ivy's departure would affect the rest of the group, but

Kayla was now convinced that it was the right thing to do. As Curtis walked through the door unaware of what was about to be shared with him, Kayla knew it was time to stick to her guns and stick by her cousin.

"So what did I miss? Did y'all order yet? I'm hungry!" Curtis said scooting into the booth right next to Ivy.

They laughed as he was always hungry! Even after just completing meal Curtis could put away more. Ivy could never understand how he kept such a small frame with as much food as he inhaled on a regular basis. His dark blue jeans were just barely staying above his backside as it met the bottom of his slightly faded Dr. Pepper t-shirt. He was still so very cute to Ivy with his caramel candy skin and wild jet black beard. But cute was as far as Curtis would ever get with Ivy. He didn't like it but it was about time he accepted it.

"We are here to talk not just for you to fill up on your fourth meal of the day," Kayla laughed.

"We can talk. We just have to eat too," he said as he gave his order to the waitress. "Besides I already know why y'all are here so we don't have that much to talk about."

"Oh, you're Psychic Friend's Network now huh?" Kayla shot back.

"Nah, not psychic just not stupid."

"So Curtis why do you think I'm here?" Ivy asked in a more serious tone.

Curtis looked her dead in the face as he answered her. "You're leaving the group aren't you?" turns out he did know.

Ivy nodded her head slightly.

"Yes I am."

"I knew this was coming soon as you agreed to marry 'Captain No Show'."

"Really Curtis?"

"May I ask you again why you want to marry that man? I mean seriously. The only thing he's consistent at is not being there for you. Is that really what you want?"

"We're not going to go through all of this again. I told you that Jack is my choice and I don't owe you or anybody else an explanation for that. All I need to know is if you're going to stick with Tank and Kayla with this music. Music is all we are here to discuss you got that?"

"Well, you quit so the music isn't your concern anymore! We got this," Curtis barked in a very disgusted tone.

"Fine."

"Fine," Curtis said getting up from the table.

He was hungry, but wasn't going to stick around for anymore of the conversation.

"I just want you to know that there are men in the world that could truly appreciate a woman like you. Men that would honor the privilege to take care of and support someone with your potential. As a friend, even though I feel like you're settling for so much less then you deserve, I'll leave it alone if that's what you want, but just know there are other men that won't leave it alone. They will come for you with every intention to queen you, and when they do, you better hope this love is strong enough or be prepared to face the fact that your boy Jack may not be the one." Curtis left the table without his food, but not before slapping down enough money to pay for all their meals plus the tip.

With her lips pursed to the side with the look of "wow" on her face Kayla decided to break the tension. "So…. that was interesting…" she said.

"I know right...Curtis never leaves the table without his food. He's really pissed," Ivy Replied.

"Ya' think?"

"So do you agree with him?" Ivy nervously asked Kayla.

"I think Curtis is just jealous and overprotective as he's always been. Yeah, so what Jack has some faults. He's human we all have them. No, I don't like how you have been left hanging out there when he hadn't shown up for you, but I also know that when he's with you, Jack brings life out of you. I've seen it myself. He loves you. He's just a lil touched that's all."

They both belted out laughter.

"Why is it that all your family and friends think I'm just never there for you? And why does Curtis know so much about our issues?" Jack shouted interrupting Ivy's recollection. "That's not cool and I feel like you feed into that then they're all looking at me crazy!"

"Jack I'm not telling them that you're a jerk and you're never there! Did you hear me say any of that?"

"So where is that coming from?"

"Because when you weren't there these are the people who were! It didn't have to be all the time, but there were enough times so that they started to be concerned about the pattern. I don't have to tell them if they see it for themselves when I'm standing there like a deer in headlights without an explanation for why you hadn't shown up!"

Dr. Gilbert interjected to try and calm them.

"Jack, you caught the part in which you sounded like the bad guy, but did you hear what Kayla said at the end of that conversation? She acknowledged all the good in you that brings out the good in Ivy so you can't just dwell on the negative. Now, Ivy, were you suspicious at all about what Curtis was saying to you?"

"No, I just know him to be like that. He gets upset and whatever he feels is just what he feels. I thought nothing of it."

"So how did Mark get into the situation?"

Ivy took a sip of the bottled water in front of her.

"A couple weeks later I got a message from him in which he stated he wanted to talk. He said he had spent about a year looking for me and so that's the least I could do."

"Were you surprised to hear from him?" Julia asked.

"Very surprised. We hadn't talked since we decided to part ways and, although it was difficult, it wasn't messy or ugly it was just a cold turkey split. I had hoped and prayed he would be happy and we both moved on."

"So why did you agree to talk to him?"

"Honestly, I was curious. I figured anybody that says they've spent that long seeking you out must have something interesting to tell you. I didn't know that he had talked to Curtis. I never would have expected that because Curtis didn't really care for Mark either from what I remember."

"So when did you find out they had talked and what had Curtis told him?"

"I just found out a couple weeks ago and when I did believe me I let Curtis have it! And I also told Mark that I didn't think it was a good idea that we continued to talk."

"Had you been seeing him as well? Like going out?" Dr. Gilbert questioned.

"We met in person once. We just went to the park, and that was the day I found out how he found me. In my mind it wasn't like going out on a date, but it was different for him and I didn't know that at first."

"When did you realize he had other intentions?"

"He told me that as long as I was happy, he wasn't around to get in between Jack and I. He then said if it didn't work out and if for any reason and I was unhappy," she paused, "He would come for me."

Jack, cringing at what he was listening to, just shook his head. If he wasn't committed to being open and saving this relationship he would have walked out.

"So you let him come for you?" Jack asked.

Although it wasn't an intentional move, Ivy had no choice but to be honest.

"Yes, I did," she confessed.

Chapter 19

Ivy had just admitted that she had opened her relationship up to invasion. Jack was furious and, to him, there was no excuse for her behavior. Even without the details of what had went on, he was shutting down and soon there wouldn't be anything he would want to say.

"I don't think I want to hear anything more. I'm done with this," Jack said.

"Jack, are you giving up?" Julia asked.

"She's giving up! She just told you she let another man in my space and where I come from that's a major offense."

"What do you mean where you come from? I don't think any one of us regardless of where we come from likes to hear that our relationship has been invaded so I'm not following you," Dr. Gilbert confessed.

"He's talking about the code of the 'streets' or the 'hood' or whatever," Ivy said rolling her eyes.

She couldn't stand it when he would reference the environmental difference in their backgrounds.

Jack always made it known that they came from two different worlds and used it as an excuse as to why Ivy didn't understand things. She felt that he kept building that barrier because it protected his ignorance. He could never just admit that he didn't understand her or just take the time to help her understand him. It put her in this very small box and it always made her the bad guy. If she would ask, "what do you mean?" or "what are you talking about?" his response was always "whatever, just forget it" or he would accuse her of acting funny when the truth was she truly did not understand what he was trying to communicate.

"You're only saying whatever because you don't understand," Jack said. "This is the kind of thing I'm talking about when I say we're just from two different worlds. Where you come maybe this kind of stuff is okay but it's not! You shouldn't have even been talking to that dude! What the hell were you doing going to the park?"

"I never said it was right! And you swear your world is so much different from mine when you grew up in church just like I did so stop acting like you don't know where I come from! You're from the same place, but you so dedicated to a past of being a 'thug' of which you never really were!"

"You don't know what I was because you weren't there!" Jack shouted.

"Fine! I don't know! Are you happy now?" Ivy shouted back. "Is that what will make you happy if I admit that I don't know about 'that life'? I am not going to apologize for not knowing how it's 'done in the streets'! I've never tried to pretend that I did! I know who I am and I've never tried to hide it from you!" Ivy continued to shout releasing months of pinned up tension. "Yes, I'm a little naïve and spoiled. Yes, I believe that there is beauty in all things and… and that all people can be good. No, I don't know how to survive in the hood, but I never tried to convince you that I did! What I do know is that understanding the differences in our cultures can make us well-rounded and… and beautiful people. I know how to illustrate life in words and make people believe in love. THAT'S WHO I AM!" she shouted. "And all I've ever asked is that you appreciate who I am because I have always done my best to appreciate who you are regardless of what or where you came from!"

It was silent.

It was the first time Ivy had ever raised her voice this loud when talking to Jack and although she didn't like it, she was glad to have gotten it out of her system. All she wanted was to be heard. For the longest time she wanted to say these things and she never imagined she would say them this way and in this place.

Jack sat quietly, angry at her, but also himself. He wasn't letting her off the hook. He didn't like the way she had spoken to him, but he never heard her talk this loud or this passionately. Jack never wanted her to feel like he didn't appreciate her when it was so far from the truth. In fact, he appreciated her innocence so much that it's the reason why he never wanted her to know about that side of his life. This was ultimately the reason he kept all the drama with Lisa away from her to begin with.

"Is this why you let Mark in?" Dr. Gilbert asked breaking the silence.

"Yes. I know it wasn't right and I'm not making excuses but, Delcoy... he spoke my language. At the time, it just felt good to be heard and understood without having to struggle to do so," Ivy confessed. "I mean, when he first started calling me we were just catching up on work related things. We didn't talk about anything personal."

Ivy was trying her best to make sure they understood that she hadn't intentionally given him more than any friend should have. They had been talking about the transitions in both of their careers and for once someone was asking her how things were going with her work. Jack rarely did because he was so consumed with his. Although Mark had told her he wasn't home to interfere with her life, he was proving that he had every intention of doing just that. She had refused to see him, so he started calling more often, sending flowers, cards, and unfortunately everything he did only magnified everything Jack wasn't doing. So she finally gave in and agreed to see him.

"And how did that play out?" Dr. Gilbert inquired.

Ivy obliged the good doctor with the explanation she had requested. She explained that her initial intention with talking to Delcoy was to find out why he had really spent a year looking for her. All the rest that had happened was not in her plan and it wasn't everything Jack had made it out to be.

Her daily routine had become pretty predictable in that she wasn't medically allowed to do too much. Jack's daughter spent Thursdays with her grandmother so she was alone all day. So she agreed to take, what she believed to be, an innocent walk in the park with Mark Delcoy on a Thursday afternoon.

Ivy, not feeling like she was doing anything wrong, didn't try to hide the fact that she was seeing him. They decided to meet at Stepping Stones Falls, a public park where anybody who knew her could have seen them. She got there a few minutes after 1 p.m. and Delcoy, who was always prompt, was already seated on a bench right in front of the falls. She took her time walking towards him and allowed herself to become engulfed in her surroundings.

It was still pretty cool, but it was a beautiful day and you could feel the magic of spring trying its best to burst through. The wind smelled of bitter fruit just starting to grow in the trees. The short blades of grass rocked side to side in rhythm with the ripples of water dancing across the pond. The earth seemed to be waving "hello" as Ivy walked down the short path leading into the park.

The moment Delcoy saw her, he lit up like a Christmas tree. No time in the last four years of his life without her had ever been as bright as this moment. She was even lovelier then he remembered her. Golden, toffee skin and thick beautiful curves that moved in all the right places with every step she took. The black and white flowered palazzo pants so neatly adorned her wide hips and the black bat-winged shirt was the perfect combination of sexy and classy.

Ivy was trying to suppress her excitement as their eyes locked. She intentionally tried to forget how attractive this man was. He stood a few inches shorter than Jack at around 5'9' and was about five shades of chocolate lighter. Delcoy was just like his favorite candy, the Reese's Peanut Butter cup, smooth and thick like peanut butter wrapped in sweet chocolate. He had hazel eyes and dark brown hair cut neatly. His goatee was nice and crispy trimmed around his full smooth lips.

Ivy started to have second thoughts about seeing him as her hormones had her very erotically charged and nearly dripping wet at just the sight or smell of a man. But, she was here now, he had seen her, and there was no turning back.

Delcoy stood up as she approached him and in his imagination he greeted her by wrapping her up in his arms and getting a handful of her full backside, but in reality he knew she wasn't going to allow it. Ivy held out her hands instead and he grabbed them with his and leaned in to kiss her softly on the cheek. As his clean shaven cheek touched hers, the smell of vanilla, jasmine and citrus enveloped his nostrils as he breathed her in. Realizing that he was holding on too long he let go and they began walking toward the water.

"Girl you smell so good! What is that?"

"It's something new I'm trying. I guess it's working for me," she said smiling.

"Yes, it is definitely working for you. I guess whoever this guy is you're seeing is working for you, too, because you are absolutely beautiful. Knocked up looks good on you baby."

She laughed. "Knocked up, huh? Well, thank you."

"So, when's the big day? You haven't said a word about this wedding. Have you set a date yet?"

Of course, Ivy couldn't answer that question so she turned the table.

"How's your wife?"

"My ex-wife is doing well. She moved to Ohio with the kids to be closer to her family, which gave me another reason to come back to Michigan so I could be closer to them. Anything else you want to know, smart ass?"

She laughed. "I see you never did get a handle on that mouth of yours."

Delcoy was lucky to get out a complete sentence without cursing. He was a true-to-form sailor and cursed like one, but he always tried to dial it down for Ivy's sake.

"I was just about to say the same thing about you," he laughed.

Ivy could have quite a smart mouth, but Delcoy always loved that about her. She was feisty and because she was so innocent and unassuming, her smart mouth was kind of sexy to him.

"Why did you want to see me Del?"

"It's been four years, I can't want to make sure you're doing ok?"

She gave him the look as if to remind him that she was no fool and knew something else was up.

"Okay, okay, I knew I was moving back here and was hoping that if you were available we could maybe pick up where we left off. You're clearly in a much more serious relationship than I imagined so I guess that's out of the question. I mean… it is out of the question right?"

She laughed. "You men never accept the possibility of it being too late do you?"

"I mean, I only slightly respect your situation so, you're right. In my mind it's not too late until you're walking down the aisle and even then you may be convinced to turn around."

"Not this time," she assured him.

Ivy turned and leaned on the concrete wall to face the water and watch the birds walk on the edge of the falls.

"I love him," she confessed.

"I'm sure you do, but does he love you?"

"Why would you assume that he doesn't?"

"I'm just asking because I know you, baby, and I know you could love a dog that refuses come home every night. Every morning you'll have a full bowl of food and water waiting for him. I know because I was that dog."

"So you think I'm stupid? Well, that's nice."

"No, I don't think you're stupid," he said grabbing her and holding her. When he noticed that she didn't struggle, he kept his arms around her and continued to speak. "I do know that you are way too nice and ridiculously naïve. You see the best in people even when it's not there. You tried to love me and I didn't let you. I ended up settling for much less and I paid dearly for it and I don't want you to settle baby girl. You, of all people, deserve to be happy."

Ivy wasn't sure how exactly to respond because she couldn't explain her confidence in the man she loved. She had never been able to quite articulate why she loved Jack the way she did, but even so, lately she wasn't happy and that, too, she couldn't explain.

"Why are you so sure I'm settling? You don't even know him," Ivy said attempting to remain confident. She wasn't trying to let Mark Delcoy see any level of vulnerability in her, but it was already too late.

"I know over the last few months since we've talked you haven't said one word about your wedding. You've talked about your book and music which only leads me to believe that these are things you're not talking to him about. Not to mention I've been holding you for the last five minutes and you haven't even tried to pull away from me."

Ivy quickly unraveled herself from his arms and turned away hoping he didn't see the tear that fell from her eye. But he had seen it and all the others that just began to flood down her face. Dell wrapped her up in his arms as both her hands were trying to wipe the tears away, but they were moving too fast for her.

"Hey... hey... hey come here baby."

"I don't know why I'm crying," she said trying to laugh it off.

"Maybe it feels good to be held."

"Maybe you just remember too much about me."

He lifted her chin and with all sincerity looked into her eyes and said, "When you love someone… you don't forget."

That phrase fell into Ivy's stomach like a ton of bricks because she couldn't understand that if Jack loved her as much as she believed, how he was always forgetting things that were important to her.

While she was mentally trying to piece things together that Delcoy kept screwing up for her, he had another plan to make her forget. With her chin still in his hand, he leaned down to kiss her hoping that maybe it would remind her of what it was like to have someone give her all the attention she needed.

"No …" she said moving her face away from his lips. Still standing in front of him she forced all the reasons she loved Jack to the front of her mind to keep her from indulging the way her flesh wanted to. He moved his head down past her face and into her neck and slowly began to kiss her right above her collarbone. Ivy shivered from the inside out. Her eyes rolled back in her head as she instantly began to imagine kisses this soft all over her body and squirming with pleasure.

She inhaled deeply, but the scent of his cologne brought her quickly back into reality. It wasn't the smell of fresh rain on rich mountain pines and smoked spices. It wasn't the Colorado Rockies and cinnamon buns. It wasn't Jack. And as turned on as she was there was still no man in the world she wanted to touch her this way, but Jack.

"I can't," Ivy said as she backed away from him.

"You know all I want is for you to be happy. You deserve that! With all you've been through, the least you deserve is someone that will love you and make you happy."

When he said those words it really struck a chord with Ivy. What did he mean when he said "with all she had been through?" It started to feel funny that he was hitting on so many points concerning the right and wrong of her present situation and reiterating what he thought she deserved. Why? He didn't know her fiancé and she hadn't shared with him in any detail the issues surrounding their present relationship. Delcoy was however making some of the same accusations about Jack's character or lack thereof that Curtis used to make. She slowly looked up at him and could tell he was avoiding her eyes.

"Look at me," she demanded.

As she had requested, he looked her right in the eyes. Delcoy knew he had said too much and could tell by her tone that she was about to search for the truth.

"Yes ma'am?"

"What do you know Delcoy?"

He hung his head down and let out a heavy sigh. She turned swiftly out of his arms and started to walk away.

Chapter 20

"Wait! Ivy!" Delcoy yelled after her. He caught up to her and grabbed her arm to try and stop her from leaving.

She snatched herself from his tight grip and shouted, "Let me go!"

"Wait!" Jack said, interrupting her story. "This man put his hands on you? Did he hurt you?"

"No, Jack he didn't hurt me. He was just trying to get me to stay and listen to him."

Jack looked sideways like he didn't believe her. He was already pissed that she had been with Mark at all. Knowing that he touched her only made matters worse.

"I promise you he didn't hurt me. Okay?"

"Jack, is it okay if she continues with the story?" Julia asked. She was far too interested in the details and didn't want to lose track.

"I guess. He shouldn't have his hands on you period!" He muttered turning back to look out the window.

So Ivy continued to explain how that she knew something wasn't right about Delcoy's approach and he was insistent on explaining how and why he had come back, but Ivy was too upset to believe a word that came out of his mouth.

"How do you know about what happened?" she yelled. "HOW!?"

"Look, it really doesn't matter how I know. What matters is that I do know and I'm worried about you girl! Do you realize what could've happened to you?"

"It does matter how you know in more ways than one! And besides you... you don't have to be worried because...because I'm fine," she stuttered. "Jack saved my life and..."

"No!" he shouted interrupting her. "Jackson put your life in danger! Don't you realize that? Had he told you the truth and kept you protected like he should have it never would have happened! If that crazy heifa had killed you it would have been his fault!"

Without thinking twice Ivy slapped Delcoy across the face. She wasn't in any way a violent natured person, but she had to shut him up. Not only was he

228

insulting, but too much of what he was saying was true and she didn't need him reminding her of that. Jack had apologized and they had made their peace with what happened. She didn't want reminders of past transgressions giving her yet another reason to be upset with Jack.

"I'm sorry...Del...I didn't mean to..."

"It's fine. I should have just told you the truth from the beginning so I'm sorry. But, I'll tell you now."

As it turned out some of the guys from the Cuban mafia who were arrested after the fallout were placed in the facility he worked in. He had only heard bits and pieces of what actually happened and thought nothing of it until he got an unexpected call from Curtis. Not being able to give details as they were all under a gag order that prevented them from sharing specific facts about the incident, Curtis only hinted to Mark that somebody he cared about was directly involved. The only mutual friend between them was Ivy and it prompted him to immediately do his own research and find out exactly what had happened.

Since he, too, worked in law enforcement, it didn't take much for him to find the case and the details therein. He had already been trying to locate her for the past six months through old phone numbers, email and social media and it hadn't worked so this was the perfect excuse to use his connections to do so, but he had no clue what he was in for.

Once he found the file he was looking for, the first picture to pop up was that of Ivy's bruised and beaten body. She laid lifeless on a stretcher in a tattered grey dress that had been ripped up to the thigh on her right side. Her arms and legs were covered in sand and blood and there was a three to four inch gash behind her left ear stretching down to her neck and oozing blood. The hair disheveled on her head surrounded her bruised face, busted lip and swollen eyes. Mark's heart dropped. There was barely any trace of the beauty that he remembered, but as he continued to read the file he realized she had indeed survived. He immediately made plans to get to Michigan to see for himself that she was okay.

Once Mark arrived in Michigan he met with Curtis who then gave him all the correct contacts for Ivy. Curtis' reasoning was simple. He may not have liked that Ivy didn't choose him, but he hated that she chose Jack. In Curtis' mind, Jack was solely responsible for everything that had happened to Ivy and he wasn't going to sit by and let her marry him. He figured if anybody could change her mind it would Mark Delcoy.

"Why was Curtis so sure that Mark could change your mind?" Dr. Gilbert questioned. She had been so engaged in the story she almost forgot that she was facilitating therapy.

"What Delcoy and I used to have was good. Curtis knew everything that I used to love about Del, Jack wasn't. So he figured having him come back around would remind me of what that was like and I'll admit it almost worked."

"Almost?" Jack asked as he turned away from the window to look at her.

"Yes, almost. I realized that Curtis was using Delcoy to manipulate me. As much as I hate to admit it, Jack you were right about Curtis."

Although he was tempted, Jack wasn't going to smile and celebrate that small victory just yet. He was still mad at her. She shouldn't have been talking to him let alone out socially with an ex-boyfriend and he didn't know about it.

"What did you get from Mark that was missing so greatly from your relationship with Jack?"

"Time," she said calmly. "When we were together even when he was busy with work or his kids, Delcoy always found a way to make me feel like the center of his world. I never made the comparison though until he came back around. That part of my life had been over and I wanted what I had with Jack."

"So you don't love him?" Dr. Gilbert asked.

"I love Jack."

"If you love me then why did you call off our wedding? Why were you with this dude? Why haven't you married me?" he shouted.

"Again, I didn't call it off I postponed it! And, I only did it because I wasn't sure if this is what you wanted!"

"Why were you unsure? Just because I missed one doctor's appointment? Seriously?" Jack shouted. He was upset that yet again his commitment was being questioned. He started pacing.

Ivy was frazzled and struggled again to get up as well. She hated his tone. When Jack was upset he had a way making her feel like she was stupid for feeling the way she felt. But, this time, she wasn't going to hold her tongue.

"You still don't get it?" she said with her hands pressing on her back.

"Get what?"

"That it's not just about a simple missed appointment. It's about your word! The idea that anything can happen in any moment and I can't trust that you will show up!"

"But you're basing this off one event! How is that fair to act like I'm so untrustworthy because one time I forget about something?"

"No not one, but one after another and after another! You get so caught up in what you think is best and what you're doing and you leave me out of your life! Even when I need you, you're off helping someone else and you expect me to just understand because it's your job! Then, you have the nerve to be offended when I tell you how inconsiderate it is!"

"You don't realize what I go through on this job! I have to see things every day that would break your heart! Every single day I put my life on the line for people that will never even know I did it. I go through a lot…"

"Everybody does Jack! You're not the only one with problems and no matter how big yours are it doesn't give you permission to devalue mine!"

"You can lower your voice I know that much," he snapped.

"Do you hear me Jack?" she asked. "Do you know how painful it is to watch you go and rescue everyone else in the world, but when I need you you're the last person to show up?! It hurts so much!" she finally admitted with tears in her eyes. "But what hurts even more is that you act as though there's nothing you can do. You act like you can't change things instead of acknowledging that you just haven't made the effort. I don't want to have to be almost dead to have your attention!" Ivy had tried to keep it together, but the tears were rolling faster than she could wipe them away. She continued, "You want me to have every confidence that you'd never do anything to hurt me, but you refuse to have the same confidence in me! The second you imagine I've hurt you, the slightest unconfirmed infraction and you erase my entire record of consistent love and support and you push me away! How is that fair?"

Jack sat shaking his head in disbelief. Where had she been storing all this frustration and why was she just now saying something?

"Why haven't you said that this is how you feel? You make it so difficult when you can just tell me stuff before you get this upset and we could've dealt with it!" Jack shouted.

Was he serious? Ivy thought to herself. She thought back on all the times she had tried to say this and never got this far because he refused to finish the conversation. Now here he was trying to simplify the process because he didn't like hearing what she had to say, in the manner in which she said it.

"Look at where we are Jack!" she shouted walking towards him. "Just telling you and hoping that you have your priorities straight is what got us here! After everything we have been through, do you understand why it's important for you to do what you say you are going to do? Anything can happen Jack! Especially with me only weeks away from giving birth to your babies, I need to be able to trust that when I call, you will answer!"

"I asked you to lower your voice!" he shouted back looking down at her.

"Wait a minute..." Dr. Gilbert interjected. They hadn't heard her as they had continued to go back and forth directly in each other's face.

"WAIT A MINUTE!" she shouted finally getting their attention.

They both took deep breaths and walked slowly away from each other in frustration.

"I'm sorry we're being rude Julia," Ivy said. She closed her eyes and took another deep breath and tried to calm herself.

"No, that's not why I stopped you. I believe in arguing and in your case this argument is about six months past due that's why it's so big. I stopped you because I want to make sure that you're hearing each other or it's all for nothing," she clarified. "Ivy... did you say, that you were only weeks away from giving birth to his babies? As in more than one?"

Chapter 21

Ivy stood there frozen like deer in headlights. She didn't realize what she had said and it was far too late to take it back. This was yet another unrevealed truth that Ivy had intentionally left out of the conversation over the last few months, but this wasn't out of fear or spite, but out of love.

Jack instantly forgot what they were just arguing about. If he understood correctly what Ivy had said, then that news just trumped everything and all things would have to take a backseat to this moment. He moved closer and looked down at Ivy as she put her head back and exhaled with her hands still pressed firmly on her back. Placing both of his hands on the sides of her tummy, he couldn't help himself from grinning from ear to ear.

"Sugar... what did you say?"

She looked up at him and smiled.

"I wanted it to be a surprise," she whispered softly.

"We're having twins?"

When Ivy nodded her head up and down, Jack stretched his arms around her back and lifted her up off the ground while he hollered in delight. He was overjoyed! Ivy knew he had hoped for twins and they had a good chance just by hereditary. Not only was Jack a twin himself, but she had twin uncles on both sides of her family. It wasn't anything they could've planned, but it's definitely something they both wanted and were very happy about.

With her feet firmly back on the floor and arms still tight around Jacks neck, Ivy hugged him tight and breathed him in as deep as she could. Tears began to fall from her eyes as she was overwhelmed with inexplicable love for this man and no matter how hard she tried she couldn't seem to shake it. It had been too long since he had embraced her this way and she missed him.

He felt her tears on his neck and each one fell like drops of love into the pool of his heart and it only made him hold her tighter. He missed her. As Jack began to softly kiss the sides of her neck and face, his hands moved up her side until he was holding the back of her head and his lips were meeting hers.

"Ahem..." Julia exclaimed with her hand over her mouth.

Jack and Ivy were slightly startled when they heard Dr. Gilbert loudly clearing her throat as they had both totally forgotten that they were in her office.

"I'm sorry Julia… I just... I'm just so excited," Jack stuttered as he stared at the woman growing his children. "So is it a boy and a girl? Two boys? Two girls? What?"

Ivy laughed. "I don't know yet, I wouldn't let them tell me. I want to wait until they get here and be surprised… again."

"I take it you were both wanting twins?"

"Well, I knew Jack did. I wasn't so sure, but when I found out I was very happy."

"When did you know?" Jack asked.

It was about two and half months ago now that Ivy went to her regularly scheduled appointment with the OB/GYN accompanied by both her mom and Kayla. Although family and friends knew she was with child, her stomach was just starting to round out making it more obvious that she was pregnant and not just fat.

As she laid back on the table, Dr. Cooper squirted the cool blue gel right across her baby bump and started the picture show. All three of them were looking at the screen trying to get a glimpse of the growing fetus when the doctor turned on the volume and they were all instantly confused.

"What's all that noise?" Ivy's mother asked. The doctor was still looking and listening with a weird look on his face and it made Ivy kind of nervous.

"Dr. Cooper is everything ok? Is something wrong?"

"Um... no nothing is wrong. The sound we're hearing is the sound of two heart beats."

"WHAT?" the three of them questioned in unison.

"Two babies?" Mother Chatman asked. "Two babies?"

"Doctor, are you sure?" Kayla asked.

Ivy just stared in disbelief. She couldn't believe what she was hearing.

"Yes, I'm sure let's look at the screen and I'll show you." Kayla and Mother Kasey turned to the screen while Ivy's eyes remained straight forward.

"Right here on the left is baby 'A' and here on the right is baby 'B' and if we turn this a little here I can tell you the sexes. Do you want to know?"

They all looked at Ivy and she was still quiet and staring straight forward. Her mom shook her arm a little to get her attention.

"Ivy, baby, the doctor is talking to you."

"I'm sorry, Dr. Cooper, did you say that there are two babies in there?"

"Yes, Ms. Ivy, you are having two babies," he laughed. "We could've seen it earlier, but one was apparently hiding behind the other. Do you want to know what they are?"

"You just told me what they are! They're two! Two babies is what they are. Two!" Ivy responded deliriously.

"Sweetie, do you want to know the sex of the babies?" her mother asked.

"No...I'll save that surprise for later. I can't even wrap my mind around the fact that they're actually two."

Ivy was complete in shock. She was in a daze about the whole thing even after they left. It wasn't until she got home and took a nice hot bath that she relaxed. Sitting there in the tub she thought about how happy Jack would be when he found out. Although she wasn't totally sure how she felt the thought of his happiness made her smile.

"Why weren't you sure?" Julia asked. Jack grabbed Ivy by the hand and sat down on the couch next to her as she began to explain.

The thought of twins is always an exciting phenomenon for people who love children, but with the recent unsettling course of events in their relationship the thought of bringing two babies into it frightened Ivy. There were times she wasn't sure if Jack would be around, for one. She figured keeping it a secret until the end would give her enough time to let things play out and her prayer was that they would still be together and Jack would get what he wanted.

"Did you really want it to be a surprise or did you feel like you couldn't tell me?" Jack asked.

"It was a little bit of both I guess."

"Why did you feel like you couldn't tell me something like this? I had been asking you about the doctors' appointments you always said your mom or Kayla was going with you."

"Only because I thought you didn't want to go. I thought you were too caught up with work and so I just let you do that."

"Sugar, do you realize how important you and our children are to me? I only work so hard at this job so that you can relax and not have to work so hard at yours?"

"I like my work though, Jack. I've only given up certain parts of it because I'm more in love with our family not because I didn't like doing it. I was always willing to give up things to support you and us, but it didn't seem like you were. How was I supposed to know you were working so hard for us when it always feels like it is for you?"

Jack stood up and paced around a little bit. He was calmer, but vulnerable and like most men not comfortable being so. He knew he hadn't been the best companion but was only doing what he knew how and had been afraid to admit he had reached the limit of what he knew how to do in a relationship. This was the first time he had the sincerest desire to be more, but didn't have the know-how.

"Jack, if there is something you feel you want to say now is the time and safe place for you to say it," Dr. Gilbert assured him.

"Do you really want to know why I work so hard?"

"Yes, baby, I do." Ivy replied.

"It's the only thing I can really do for you!" He shouted with his hands in the air. Jack finally admitted his biggest insecurity.

Jack knew if he was good at anything it was at being a police officer. Even after his nephew was kidnapped, something in him rose to the occasion and for three years he worked nonstop until he brought him home. His work gave him the validation he needed to know he was contributing something positive back into the world. After meeting Ivy she only motivated him to do it that much better. In everything she did she had a way to making it look so effortless but in spite of her work ethic, Jack knew when she was worn and when she was tired or frustrated. He wanted to be her restoration, but the only way he knew how, other than physically loving her, was to work hard and serve more so that she would be proud and wouldn't have to worry if somebody loved her enough to let her rest.

"You will never understand what it was like wondering whether or not you would make it off that island. Sometimes I can't get the image of you on that beach out of my head. It was my fault that all that horror happened to you and most days it's hard to watch you take care of me knowing that I don't deserve to be with you."

That was mouthful that Ivy never thought she'd hear come out of Jack.

"Jack you have to realize that the only person to blame for what happened to Ivy was Lisa. Once you chose Ivy there was nothing Lisa wouldn't do to change your mind and her goal was to rob you of any happiness you could possibly have without her. Now she's gone and you are letting her rob you of your happiness by holding on to guilt that doesn't belong to you," Dr. Gilbert explained. "And, when it comes to things we deserve, just consider this, none of us deserve salvation, but God gives it freely. So, if you believe that God has given Ivy to you then you have to know that it's not about what you deserve, but what you're willing to accept."

He came back over to the couch and sat next to Ivy and looked her in the eyes.

"My work is all I know how to do to provide for our family and be a good man. I admit it, I never learned how to do relationships very well which is why they all went down in flames, but you are the only woman I have ever believed was worth fighting for. Sometimes I think you're just too good for me, Sugar, but I do believe that God gave you to me," he said sincerely. "I didn't know it was that important to you for me to be at all the things I missed. All I had was brothers growing up and my mother didn't have a career that we needed to support. So I don't know how to recognize when you need that from me. All I know how to do is work hard and come home to you," he sighed, "… the rest… you have to teach me Sugar."

Ivy let out a great sigh of relief. All she needed to hear was that this, indeed, is where he wanted to be and was willing to do the work. He had never let her hear any of these words, which is why it was so hard for her to know what to have hope in. Most of his actions were saying that he didn't have time for her while the truth is that time was the one thing he wasn't sure how to give. Dr. Gilbert wasn't too amazed from seeing this same issue with so many prior to these two. The truth is that many people in troubled relationships only need to talk to each other, honestly and in the same language.

"This is a major breakthrough for you both. You're finding how safe it really is for you to let your guards down and be honest about how you really feel. Don't you feel better now knowing that you can actually trust each other enough to tell each other the truth?" Julia asked.

Jack grabbed Ivy's hand and they locked their fingers together and nodded in agreement of what Dr. Gilbert had suggested. Although it had been difficult to get here and they still had a long way to go. It felt really good to finally get these things out and know that at the end of it all they were still more in love with each other than anything that would try to separate them.

"Good. Now your next session is next Tuesday, but before then, you have an assignment and some exercises I want you to start doing. The first exercise that I want you to do is get in the habit of being more deliberate about telling each other when something is wrong or is bothering you. Ivy, you especially have to stop letting fear prevent you from speaking your truth, and all doors that were and are still open that would invade this relationship must be closed."

"Yes, ma'am," she agreed.

"And, Jack, you've got to start learning how to speak her language. Now that you know what it is, remember being home by a certain time everyday doesn't work if you don't create space to be attentive to her. She's worked all day, too, working on her book, taking care of Melanie and preparing for you to come home, so she also needs that space with you to unwind."

"Yes, ma'am, I will work on that," he agreed.

"Now your joint assignment," she began, as she looked at them both above those big, round glasses. This was the speech she had been waiting to give them and meant for them to hear and understand every word.

"Together, you need to set a date for your marriage. Your marriage, not wedding! Marriage is not about the wedding. It's not about who can be there and who can't, when or where, colors or tuxes and all the other crap that has made getting married a billion dollar business. It marks the end of your journeys alone as two single individuals and the beginning of your life as one in the eyes of God. There is officially nothing and no one else more important than what you have together. Not another decision in your life should be made without each other in mind. Everything takes a backseat in that moment when you say 'I do' and you dedicate your life's purpose to each other's happiness and well-being. The child you have, and the children you're about to have although you love them with all your heart, they will come second to this union. There will be plenty of times when that will be a hard pill to swallow, but when the children are gone, it'll just be you and there has to be enough strength there to keep this alive when everything else goes away."

Julia sat down on the table in front of them, grabbed their hands that were still clasped together and looked at them with all sincerity. "Remember this, God is love. So anything dedicated to love and to God becomes the most powerful thing in your world. The other side of that coin is that anything you place above this union in place of love or in place of God, you give the power to destroy everything you have built."

Chapter 22

Dr. Gilbert had given Jack and Ivy so much to think about. There was so much about their relationship that, before now, they thought they had a handle on only to discover they had been placing a cover on many of their true feelings. Not so much feelings of anger and deception, but just being afraid to admit how much they needed each other to get through what they had been through. One of the areas where they were alike was being too stubborn and proud to be vulnerable. If this was going to work, they both had to do a lot more trusting, not only in each other, but also if they believed that it was God's divine order that they be together, they needed to trust Him.

As they stood in the parking lot of the office park, they were both thinking very intensely about the words the good doctor had said to them. They stopped in front of Jack's car, looking oddly at each other trying to figure out how to break the silence.

"So what do you have planned for this evening?" Jack asked Ivy.

"Not much. You?"

"Well, Mel is with my parents for the weekend and I would like to take you to dinner if that's okay?"

"Jack Benett, are you asking me out on a date?"

"If I am, are you saying yes?"

"Maybe," she teased

"Oh yeah?" he laughed. "What would it take to convince you?" Jack asked as he got closer to her.

He turned her around and held onto her and she rested her head back on his chest. Ivy closed her eyes as he placed his arms around her and laid his hands on her tummy.

"You know we could skip dinner and just go home. We have quite a bit of making up to do…" he suggested.

"Ummmm…" was all she could get out of her mouth in response to him.

"Is that a yes?"

Ivy turned around and grabbed his face and kissed him softly on his lips. "As much as I'd love to… your children are hungry," she teased.

"You play too much," he said laughing. "Okay well get in the car and let's go," he instructed.

As she turned around and he slapped her on her full bottom. She jumped quickly turning back around and trying to hit him back playfully.

"Come on stop playing get in the car," he said opening her door.

Ivy followed instructions and they went on their way. It worked out that Kayla had dropped her off because she wasn't supposed to be driving anymore. She hadn't expected that she would be leaving the session with Jack, but she wasn't complaining. It was nice to be able to return to the place where being in love just felt good and not complicated. Although they both knew that everything about love isn't fun all the time, they knew it also shouldn't be overrun with frustration and anxiety. Everything needed balance and sometimes we need a little help getting back to the middle.

Ivy sat smiling, seated comfortably across from Jack in the big corner booth of Blackstone's Pub downtown. She had a great meal and great company. It had been a tough one, but any day she ended with Jack was a good day for her.

"You realize how long it's been since we've been out on a date?" Ivy asked.

"It hasn't been that long has it?"

"Yes, it has. I mean real dates when we went out and did something that wasn't work or business related. Our schedules used to be so crazy. It was always easier to cook at home and watch a movie."

"I thought you liked being at home though," Jack replied.

"I did until it started being your nap time," she laughed. "Not that I don't like being at home, but I like this when we both have each other's attention and you can't just fall asleep on me."

"Be honest with me, Sugar?" he said seriously. "What is it about my job that makes you so insecure in our relationship?"

She sighed.

"When it comes to your job… you always have this sense of urgency to make things happen. It really is like you're Batman and I love and admire how passionately you rush off to the rescue, but I guess… I guess I was disappointed when you didn't have the same urgency about us. You would get home and be so tired and sleepy and I started to think that I wasn't enough to keep you excited. Sometimes I just needed you to want to be with me and that be enough."

"You really think you're not enough?" he questioned.

"That's how it felt sometimes."

Jack shook his head and laughed.

"If you only knew... Sugar, I couldn't do what I do on that job everyday if I didn't have you to come home to. Knowing that I have you is what gets me through my day."

"Really?" she smiled.

"Really, really."

"I'm sorry about Delcoy... I knew what I could be opening myself up to and I was wrong. Even if you didn't listen I should've tried harder to talk to you," Ivy admitted. "But when you didn't show up that day... in my mind nothing was going to matter to you until it came through a 911 call. I don't want to be your case. I want to be the lady you share your life with, not the one whose life you're always trying to save."

"Hmm..." he nodded. "I'm sorry, Sugar," he said shaking his head. "Like I said, I didn't know it was that important to you. I had no idea that one thing I did or didn't do could send so many other signals that aren't the least bit reflective of what you to mean to me," he said grabbing her hand from across the table. "I never knew what I needed in life until I met you and I cannot, and do not, intend to live without you. I love you, girl."

Ivy put her head down as a solitary tear rolled down her face.

"Do you hear me?"

She looked up at him and nodded her head up and down.

"I'm serious. I love you."

"I love you," she whispered through the tears.

They were slightly interrupted as the bus boy came to clear their table. Jack handed her a napkin and she wiped her eyes. She took a deep breath and grabbed a small bottle of sanitizer from her bag and cleaned her hands. Jack got up and helped her scoot out of the booth and up into his arms.

"Okay. Can we go home now?" she asked.

"Sure, I'll take you home. Your mom is probably worried about you now anyway."

"No… I want to go to our home. Together," she clarified.

"You're the boss Sugar," Jack said grinning. He placed his arm around her and walked her outside.

The home Jack had moved into alone was one that Ivy had picked out. The three bedroom family ranch style home now looked like a bachelor's pad due to Jack being left to his own devices. Ivy walked in to find empty laundry baskets in the living room next to a pile of dirty clothes on the sofa. There were shoes in every corner of the room. The table was covered with paperwork and the sink full of dishes. She looked around and just laughed. Knowing Jack, it would be at least two more days of this before he had a cleaning spell and the whole place reeked of bleach. He knew Ivy was looking at his mess, but didn't try at all to cover his plight he instead playfully blamed her.

"You see what happens when you leave me alone?" he teased.

"Yeah, I can only imagine what you've done to our bedroom," she said marching down the hall.

"Umm… Sugar, you may not want to go back there just yet," he said following her.

Jack stood at the door scratching his head as she laid her eyes on his shame. What a surprise, she thought when she saw there in the middle of his bed was his computer, chargers, his glasses that he never wore and two of her scripts. He couldn't stand it when she brought her work to bed and here it was he had been spending his nights glued to the computer working and then reading her work for entertainment.

"Well, well, well!" she teased. "So now who's bringing their work to bed huh?"

"Listen, it's not the way I'd prefer to be busy in this room, but it just happened. Don't judge me," he said as he began to move the piles of work off of their bed.

"Oh no! You used get on my case about this. *Lady what is all this stuff in the bed? Do you have to do all that clickin' and clackin' while I'm tryna sleep? What are all these papers? What are you doing with all this stuff?*" she laughed mocking him. She sat down on the bed and picked up one of her scripts.

"Since when are you reading my stuff?"

"Since I haven't had you around much to talk to. I figured maybe if I read some of the stuff you wrote it would help me figure you out."

"Did it?"

"A little bit."

"Oh yeah?" she laughed. "What did you find out?"

He sat down on the bed next to her.

"Honestly I didn't realize how good you were. I was kinda sleeping on your skills," he laughed. "But um… I love your leading lady in this one because she's just like you."

"How do you mean?" Ivy questioned.

She had written much of herself into her work, but she had never heard him make the connection.

"She's strong, confident, and sexy, but still sweet, innocent, and lovable. Just wanting time and attention, not caught up in material things and simply hoping her presence makes a difference in the world. That's just like you."

Ivy was surprised at how well he had interpreted her writing and found her inside. Thinking about how well he had just articulated his findings, she shook her head and smiled. She quietly got up and went to the middle drawer of the dresser to grab some pajamas. Many of her things she had put away in the house since it was her intention to move in the same time Jack did. Lucky for her some of her basic needs were still there. Unfortunately, some of the things she had there weren't going to fit over her breast and those babies.

Ivy gave up and grabbed one of Jack's old, oversized t-shirts and put it on. Due to his sad laundry skills, this one had been stretched just enough to make it down to her knees. While she was changing Jack noticed a thick black strap on her right thigh and wanted a closer look.

"Come here," he instructed.

"What?"

Still sitting on the edge of the bed, he watched her walk back over to him. She stood motionless between his legs as he started to slide his hand up under her shirt.

"Hey...hey, be careful now," she laughed.

They had agreed and committed to not having sex again until after they were married and Ivy knew she couldn't be tempted in her condition. Jack didn't say a word until he reached the strap and he was not happy. He quickly unfastened the holster from her thigh and sat it on the bed.

"Tell me what you're doing pregnant with twins with a gun strapped to your leg!"

"Jack, calm down, it's perfectly safe. You know I'm licensed to carry this and I've been trained, by you in fact so what's the big deal?"

"The big deal is that you're pregnant and you shouldn't have this on you!"

"My being pregnant is the perfect reason for me to have this on me! You think I'm not going to be prepared if another wacko decides they want to hurt me?"

"Okay, okay, listen…" he said calming himself and trying to calm her.

He noticed how quickly she got upset and he didn't want to further frustrate her. He grabbed her by her hips and pulled her close to him.

"I get it Sugar, you're scared, but you can't let this fear change who you are. You hear me?" she looked down into his eyes and nodded. "You are sweet and you are kind. You don't have to change that to prove to anybody that you can take care of yourself. Now, I don't mind if you want to carry this, but I don't want it on your body you understand?"

She let out a deep sigh and hesitantly agreed.

"Hey..." he said playfully slapping her backside. "I'm serious girl. If, by chance, you do need it, in your condition it can be too tricky to try and manipulate this weapon while it's on you like that."

"Okay Jack. I hear you."

Although Ivy had begun to feel a better sense of security knowing that her Glock 19 was right on her side, she understood Jack's concern and so would oblige his instruction. As long as she felt safe, she would honor his request.

Chapter 23

They were both in bed clothes, which they normally didn't wear, and so made themselves as comfortable as possible as they prepared to sleep for the first night together in their bed, in their own home. Jack slid down and nestled himself against her billowy chest and grinned big as he placed his hand on her stomach. He rubbed it back and forth hoping to catch any movement of his babies.

"I still can't believe there are two babies in there," he said.

"I can. Sometimes it feels like they're just walking around like full grown toddlers in there," she laughed.

"Walking around huh?"

"Yes! Your children rarely stay still. They're sleeping now, thank God!"

"Do you sing to them?"

"Yes, I do, and as soon as I start they get to moving."

"For real? Do it now, let me see?" Jack said getting excited. He had missed moments like this. He liked being able to be near her and talk to his babies and feel them moving.

"Baby, I'm so tired I don't want them waking up."

"Please!" he begged, raising his chin to kiss her neck. "Besides I miss your voice."

"Okay, okay, just a little bit."

She started to sing *Beautiful Surprise* by India Arie and half way through the first verse sure enough the babies started moving. Jack sat up with his hand still firmly pressed on her tummy and begged her to do it again and again. Although he was beyond excited and enjoying the show, he knew she was tired. He finally let her rest and laid back down and let her turn into him just the way she always did.

"Sugar…"

"Yeah, babe?"

"Why do you love me?"

She giggled a little and he let his arms go from being tightly wound around her.

"That's funny?"

"No!" she whined. "Come back here," she demanded pulling him back closer to her. "I just knew you were going to ask me that is all."

"Okay, well tell me. I really want to know. I mean… I know you do, but I need to know why."

The truth was that Ivy had plenty of preconceived notions about love before Jackson Taylor Benett burst into her life. The sad part was that she really thought that she had it understood, only to find out, in a very tough way, that she was wrong. She had understood love to be like some sort of magic because of how it made people feel and the power that it had to strip control from every instinct humans believed they could regulate themselves.

It wasn't until she lost her best-friend David to cancer that she had a rude awakening. Most of her pain stemmed from disappointment because she felt like her love didn't have the power to save his life and she interpreted that as a failure in her own ability. Ivy felt flawed and incapable, but what she hadn't realized was how strong her love truly was, because it had the power to let him go.

Love wasn't an enchanted magic act that could wield the universe into doing what we wanted it to, but rather a conscious choice of submission. Giving up your own power and surrendering to God's will even when it hurts. If they were indeed created to love Jack, as divine partners in life, no matter what chaos life brought to their table, if they surrendered to it, love could prevent them from wanting and being anything but the best for each other.

"Jack… loving you has been the most humbling experience of my life. I love you because … because I can," she answered.

It wasn't complicated, deep or profound, but Jack understood exactly what she meant and he agreed with her sentiment completely. It wasn't a statement of arrogance nor one to deemphasize all that they meant to each other, but that they simply had the capacity to do all that would come with loving each other. By the grace of God, they finally understood that because of love, they each embodied the power to continuously forgive one another, have patience with one another, and strengthen one another.

This love offered the gift of sight beyond their faults, into the desires of their hearts and even into the future to embrace the people they would become. It was humbling. A marvelous act of submission that resembled the freedom of embracing the wind that carried the wings of eagles. This is why people in love feel like they can fly. Giving love gives us the weightless feeling of immortality because its authority goes beyond our own human strength. To choose to love someone daily, so selflessly, and without any obligations is liberation from the very boundaries of humanity. To love simply because you can is the great privilege to experience immortality in this mortal life.

He kissed her forehead and smiled. He asked God for nothing in his prayers tonight, but thanked Him for everything he had.

"I'm safe with you right Jack?" she asked in a soft whisper.

"Of course, you are, Sugar" he felt her tighten her grip on him and wondered why she asked such a question when she already knew the answer. Nevertheless, not a minute passed after and she was sleeping peacefully and he followed suit.

Jack could snore like nobody's business, but he was still somehow a very light sleeper so Ivy's constant moving was making it a little difficult to rest. Ivy normally slept still and in one spot so this moving was not something he was used to, but Jack figured it was only due to the extra weight from the babies and she was having a hard time getting comfortable. He turned her over on to her left side and figured that would help. There was no way he could've known what was really going on inside her head that was keeping her restless.

The unconscious Ivy was back inside that hotel room in Cuba. The rain started to pour, the thunder started rolling in and with one crackling flash of lightening, the power went off and the room was covered in darkness. Scrambling in the room for her cell phone with only the light of the moon and flashes of lightening to guide her, she found the phone in the bed between the sheets. As soon as she had the phone in her hand, it began to ring loudly startling her as there was no caller identification available. In the dark room with nothing but the eerie telephone ringing and wind pressing against the hotel walls, Ivy stared at the phone unsure if she should answer. She was alone and would soon need help if the power didn't come back on so she nervously slid her finger across the touchscreen and answered.

"Jack?" she whispered with hope.

"Tsk, tsk, tsk, you still hoping for my Jack to show up? Well, we both know that's not gonna happen," Lisa said with every intent to torment Ivy.

Ivy found herself looking around the room as if she knew she wasn't alone and backing into the door.

"What do you want you sadistic witch?" Ivy snapped.

"Only what is mine, *ladrón*!" Lisa growled viciously.

"I'm not a thief! Jack chose me!"

"That he did, but we all make bad choices in life and that was one of his. Unfortunately, you will have to pay for it."

"What do you want from me?!" Ivy screamed.

"Revenge!"

Before Ivy could respond all she heard was the dial tone. The phone was frozen black, she couldn't make any calls or send any texts for help and the dial tone wouldn't stop. She turned quickly to open the door only to discover that she was locked inside. Ivy was desperately grasping at the doorknob until the door itself was shaking, but there was no way the door would open without a much stronger force then her own. With her hands shaking intensely she tried the phone again, but to no avail. The only other way out of the room was the patio doors to the beach, but before she could reach the door something hit her bluntly on the back of her head and she was falling to the floor.

Ivy tried to focus her eyes and with blurred vision all she could see was Lisa and her brother, Sammie, soaking wet from the rain outside, standing over her. With her black mascara running from her eyes, Lisa, with one leg on each side of Ivy, looked down at her victim. Lisa lightly patted Ivy's face with her cold hand as streams of blood began to slide down Ivy's cheek from the glass in her head. Ivy's instinct was to attempt to trip Lisa and fight back, but something was holding her down. She was paralyzed and at the mercy of her enemy and there was nothing she could do.

"Wake up, mama," Lisa taunted. "You thought it was all over didn't you?" she asked with her swift rolling accent attempting to pierce more fear in to Ivy's heart.

"I told you Jack was mine!" she yelled, and with all her strength kicked Ivy repeatedly in the ribs. "I told you *no hay finales felices*!" Lisa yelled.

She continued to shout in English and Spanish that there would be no happy ending for Ivy and between every insult there was more kicking until Ivy was howling in agony. Finally, out of breath, Lisa stood up straight and fixed her clothes.

"Take her to the beach." Lisa commanded her brother.

Sammie grabbed Ivy by her arms and started dragging her across the floor following Lisa's instructions that she continued to bark in Spanish to take Ivy's beaten body towards the ocean. She opened the patio doors and, as Ivy's bottom went over the base of the door, the grey dress ripped leaving tattered pieces in the bottom of its base. The carpet underneath her that had roughly burned her soft brown skin turned into sand that started to cut into her like glass. Every move she made in an attempt to free herself only made the pain worse so Ivy stopped struggling. Instead she slowly closed her eyes and let her prayers drown out her five senses that had magnified the storm around her.

In her head she repeated over and over, *Jesus! Jesus! Please don't let me die here! Not like this!* By the time she got to the seventh repetition of her weak and desperate prayer she started to feel the sand under her body get cold and gooey. They were at the edge and she could feel the water start to splash against her side as her arms were released and fell lifelessly onto the sand. Assuming she was dead, they left her there and she felt their steps getting further and further away from her.

Ivy waited. She waited until she no longer heard voices or felt feet moving across the gritty wet sand and there was nothing left than the peaceful sound of ocean. The rain had eased and was only softly falling on her face. She opened her eyes and could only look up to see the sky painted grey with bright streaks of silver flashes whipping between the clouds.

Every part of her body hurt and Ivy knew she was losing blood, but she didn't know from where and she couldn't move anything. With the tide rushing in, she could feel the water starting to push and pull her body against the edge of the beach. The storm above wasn't finished and, if she didn't move herself, the water was going to pull her body out into a rough ocean. With the little bit of strength she had left Ivy called for help, but her faint cries were drowned out by the booming thunder.

Her only hope was to remain calm and let her body float until someone found her so she let herself drift into the water. It was quiet...and the water got still ... and Ivy knew that it was a bad sign. Still waters this close to the shore only meant that a wave was building beneath her and being unable to move meant that she would drown.

Accepting that these may be her final moments Ivy began to think of all the things she never got to do and tears began to fall from her eyes and into the now, slow-rolling ocean. There wasn't much in her life that she regretted, but many things she still wanted to do. Overall, she was satisfied with all the things she had done. Her only regret at this moment was that she didn't get a chance to see if she was in fact carrying the child of the man she loved. The most she could do is get her hands to the top of her stomach and pray that if she had to die that there was no baby that would die with her. In the chance that it was, she wanted to at least let him or her know how much she loved them.

"If you're in there little one..." she whispered in a faint, raspy voice, "I love you".

She thought she heard something in the distance, a voice calling her. Ivy, delirious from blood loss, closed her eyes and assumed God was calling her home… until it got louder. It was Jack screaming her name.

"IVY!!!!... IVY, NOOOOOOOOOOO!!!" he screamed.

Before she could muster the strength to answer his calls the wave that had been so quietly building beneath her was now standing 4ft above her ready to crash over her weak body. The same water she had embraced her entire life was now pounding onto her like stones and carrying her body under the sea. With water rushing into her mouth, nose, and ears, her lungs began to fill with fluid, she began to lose consciousness, but she could still faintly hear Jack calling her name.

"Ivy! Ivy!!"

Seconds later a gasping Ivy woke up from her nightmare in a panic to Jack rocking her back and forth, patting her face and pleading with her to wake up. This scenario was all too familiar with him as well and it scared him to imagine what she was suffering because he certainly didn't want to re-live his scariest moments on that beach. Disoriented, she looked around to see things that were familiar and began to find comfort that she had only been dreaming.

"Ivy, you're okay! Calm down. You're okay," he said, trying his best to calm her.

"Where am I?" she questioned.

"You're home, baby. We are at home."

In relief, she frantically grabbed Jack and held on to him and cried simultaneous tears of anxiety and joy. Although Ivy was relieved that she was safe at home, the pictures in her mind had tormented her sleep were and were so frightening and unnerving. She was comforted that Jack was there, holding her, rocking her gently, assuring her that she would be okay.

"Was it Cuba? The nightmare?" Jack asked with distress.

"How... how did you know?" she said still panting. As her breathing pattern gradually began to regulate, Jack laid her back down on her back and cuddled her.

"Your mother told me," he confessed.

Mother Kasey had called Jack the first night she lost consciousness after having this night terror and shared with him what had been going on. Ivy wouldn't tell Jack but her mother felt he had a right to know.

"I didn't want you to worry. I didn't want you to think I was crazy."

"Shhh... no, baby, I don't think you're crazy," he assured her as he held her tighter. "I think you're scared, but I'm here and I'll always be here and nothing will happen to you. I promise."

"It was so real!" she cried, "It's always so real."

"It's over, Sugar, okay... It's over and you're safe now."

Jack held onto her as tight as he could without squishing the babies. He had no idea this is what she had been going though and regretted every night she had spent without him. He was just as scared of losing her in that moment as he had been on that island, but he couldn't rescue her the same way. Jack knew all he could do was be there and pray for her and that's exactly what he was determined to do until the nightmares stopped.

Ivy unraveled herself from Jack's tight grip and got out of the bed to get her purse.

"Where are you going?"

"I have something for you." She grabbed a brown envelope and wobbled her way back to the bed. She slid back into the bed and sat back up against the black, leather-padded headboard. Still breathing heavily and trying to calm herself, she crossed her short legs at the ankle, sat back, and handed Jack the envelope.

"What is this?"

"Open it, babe," she said with tears still in her eyes and a serious look on her face.

Jack sat up, opened the envelope and when he read the document in his hands he was pleasantly surprised.

"Is this for real?" he asked.

"As real as it gets," she replied.

In that envelope was their marriage certificate that she had acquired by faith when they first started therapy a few weeks ago. She had said to herself that if she could make it through a night after that nightmare and Jack was still by her side that would be all the confirmation she needed. They had seven days before it expired and she was finally sure in this moment that this was what she wanted.

"When?" he asked.

"I don't want to wait another day. I don't need any of the other stuff that comes with a wedding. Dr. Gilbert was right. This is about you and me. We may not be perfect, but we're perfect for each other and I don't need an audience. Let's go to your parents' house tomorrow and have your dad marry us."

Chapter 24

The Michigan winter has always had its way of holding on as long as it possibly could. Just last week it had reached a very comfortable 60 degrees with the promise of spring and now, today, Friday, April 4th, the evening Jack and Ivy would say their vows, it was back down to 32 degrees. Luckily for them it was nice and warm inside the home of Jack's mother and father where they would stand and commit their lives to one another.

It worked out that Ivy's brother and his family were in town for a visit so all of their siblings were able to attend. Both families had spent the entire day preparing for this impromptu ceremony and they were all finally inside one house getting ready to witness this much anticipated union.

Ivy was upstairs in one of the guestrooms with her sisters, her mother, mother-in-law to be and Kayla, trying her hardest to stop crying so she could get her make-up on. She was so excited that the day had finally come and it was a different feeling than she had before when preparing. Now she was fully aware of the work it was going to take to make a lifetime promise and the thought that she was truly ready and willing to face it with no inhibitions meant that she had finally conquered her fear of commitment. She was proud of herself and her hormones were in overdrive and so she couldn't stop crying.

"Ivy your make-up is not going to get done like this," Ivory laughed.

"Listen, you wanna carry these babies and see how well you hold tears in?" Ivy said laughing. She took a deep breath and decided to try again. "Okay I think I'm ready this time."

Kayla began again to work on her make-up as Ivy's mother and sister, Ivonne, worked on her hair. Melanie came running into the room all dressed in a lavender dress of lace and bows that her grandma Adele bought her for Easter. Who knew she'd be wearing it for her father's wedding.

"Movy, I need braids!" she yelled out. Ivy sometimes braided her hair and when she did Melanie felt so fancy. She would put on her princess dresses and twirl around in the mirror just so she could see her braids swinging. She didn't realize her daddy was getting married, but knew this dress meant the occasion was special enough for braids.

"Okay, Mel, go get your chair."

"Did she call you Movy?" Kayla asked.

"Isn't it cute?" Mother Benett said. "We were trying to help her say 'Mom Ivy' and all she got was 'Movy'." She laughed. It was indeed very cute. The adorable three-year-old had embraced Ivy very well as her full-time mom and that was a blessing. So while Ivy was getting her hair done by her mother, Melanie was sitting in her little chair in front of Ivy getting her braids.

Jack was downstairs with his four brothers getting dressed and talking about the babies.

"So, Jackie, do you have to do everything so intense?" Jason joked. "You couldn't just have one baby you had to have two at the same time?"

"Listen, man, I'm not complaining I got everything I want, double the diapers and all. Don't be a hater, bro," he laughed.

"Nah, you can have that, my man. I'm praying for you, bruh."

"Please do that because I will need it," Jack said, fixing his tie in the mirror. Once it was perfect he turned and faced them. "But, seriously, um... I'm glad my brothers are here. I couldn't imagine a better group of men to stand with me today. I know this thing with Ivy has been a wild ride, but having you all with me to support us means everything to me."

"You're the baby boy, Jackie, I told you we got your back no matter what. You've made us proud man," Jupiter declared.

Ivy's brother, James Jr. came into the room with her god-son Manny to congratulate the groom. Manny held out his hand and Jack shook it and pulled him in for a hug. The two had gotten quite close over the last couple years and Manny was glad his god-mother had someone like Jack to look after her.

"I'm glad you're here man." Jack said to James Jr.

"Aw, man, I wouldn't miss it. I expect nothing but the best from the man that is going to marry my baby sister. Any man with the balls to talk my dad he way I heard you did has my respect," he said, shaking

Jack's hand. "Take care of her, Jack. I'm not cop but I am certified you understand?" he joked.

"I totally understand," Jack laughed. "I will take care of her."

"So, Jackie," Jasper said, "You about ready to do this?"

"Yes, sir!" he said buttoning his suit coat. "Let's do this."

With nothing to rush them, they had taken their time preparing for this evenings ceremony. Ivy's sisters had decorated the living room with as many purple and white flowers as they could find that day. Along with a roaring fire behind the steel black gated fireplace, there were candles lit all over the room and all the normal bulbs in the lamps were replaced with purple ones making for a very romantic setting. For Jack and Ivy it would be one of the most memorable events of their lives and even though it had only taken a day to plan, it felt like so much longer. It wasn't about what was perfect it was simply about what was right, necessary and divine for the sake of their happiness.

It was now nine o'clock in the evening and Jack stood at the bottom of the stairs alongside his four brothers and the rest of their family waiting for his bride. He was dressed in Ivy's favorite two button grey suit, complete with vest and a dark purple and silver paisley tie and handkerchief. The song that played was *'When I First Saw You'* from the Dreamgirls soundtrack. Jack fought the tears that begin to fall down his deep, chocolate-skinned face when he looked up and saw his little lady. She was at the top of the stairs in a long sleeve cream dress with purple swirls that covered her from collarbone to foot. It lightly hugged her full figured body and around the big baby bump with grace. Jack couldn't think of any better way to see his bride. Her beautiful brown hair was up in a bun surrounded with beautiful purple roses that accented the gold in her eyes. She was truly his dream.

    Ivy held tightly to the cherry wood banister and slowly walked down the burgundy carpeted stairs in silver slippers to meet her groom. He grabbed her hand at the last step and guided her gently towards him. Jack and Ivy stood face to face holding hands in the center of the living room ready for Jack's father, Pastor Benett, to lead them through their vows. Just before he began, the doorbell rang.

Everyone looked at each other and chuckled in confusion as everyone that was supposed to be there was already there. Pastor Benett gave Jupiter the nod to go and answer the door. As he walked toward it everyone's eyes followed in curiosity as to who could be interrupting this private affair. Jupiter opened the door and there stood Agent James Kasey. Ivy's father had come to her wedding.

All the Kasey girls stood there in shock as none of them expected to see their father standing there at the door.

"Daddy?" Ivy said with tears in her eyes.

"I'm sorry I'm late, baby girl," he said as he walked inside towards her. Without even thinking she rushed into her father's arms crying tears of joy.

Jack had called him early that morning and strongly suggested he get the next flight out of D.C. and into Flint. The newest agent in the FBI had kept his part of the bargain and was determine to make sure that Agent Kasey kept his. No matter what it took, if his baby girl was getting married, he was not going to miss it.

Now they stood again, immediate family complete, in the center of the living room with all parents, all siblings, little Melanie, Kayla and Tank ready to complete their vows. Although they had both agreed the traditional vows would suffice for them, they had some additional things they wanted to add in consideration of what they had both been learning in therapy.

"Jackson Taylor and Ivy Lynn both have something they would like to share at this time," Pastor Benett announced, in his deep, raspy voice. "Miss Ivy, you may go first."

Before she could even get started, Kayla handed her one of their grandfathers handkerchiefs because she knew Ivy wouldn't get through it without shedding a tear.

"You all know me and therefore know how much I love Batman. You probably don't know why and I'll admit myself I never thought I'd actually meet him and be able to express my love to him. Before you, Jackson Taylor Benett, came into my life I was that girl who was very cynical about love. I was dismissive to the idea that if by chance I obtained it, it would have the legs strong enough to stand forever.

I was more familiar with the infallible nature of man and overwhelmed with the fact that just because someone loved you… didn't mean that they would stay with you. That lack of faith was a darkness that I didn't know I was in and couldn't get out of alone. Batman always represented, to me, a champion that finds one in the darkness and courageously brings one into the light. Jackson, you are my champion," she cried.

"You embraced me in a very dark place and have rescued me in more ways than one! Your love has brought me into the brightest lights and has inspired me to fight for this space where I now believe wholeheartedly that some things can last forever," she paused and took and deep breathe.

"Should the day ever come again that we are surrounded by death and doubt, I promise to speak only life and hope." She took the hanky and wiped her eyes. "My love, you are the undisputed heavy weight champion of my heart and today I commit to you the very best of me. I promise that nothing and no one will ever have access to the space in my heart where you dwell."

It didn't take much of her voice to bring the mighty Jack to tears so no one was surprised that he wasn't even trying to hold them back. His twin, Jordyn, placed his hand on his shoulder as he understood, more than anyone, that although they were all strong men, Jack had gone through a lot to finally have this woman in front of him saying her vows. Now, if he could just make it through his own, he would be happy. He was nowhere near as eloquent with words and articulate as she was, but he would be honest and direct with no hesitation.

"Ivy, over the last few years you've made my life bigger, brighter and more meaningful than I ever imagined. It's hard for me to put into words how much I appreciate you and what you really mean to me and just saying I love you isn't enough in this moment. There are lots of promises I'd love to make, but letting you down is something I've done before. I realize now that it takes more than words for a man to keep his word.

Today, I make these promises to God, ask you to hold me accountable and pray that I have the courage and wisdom on how to keep them. I promise God that when you need me, I will be there. I promise God that when you call me, I will answer. I promise God that no one will celebrate you more than I will. I promise God that I will protect you and provide for you. I'll be a good husband, a good father, a good friend and a great leader for our family.

My commitment to you, Sugar, is that I will stay committed to God, so that when I fail, you can see past my faults and see the God in me and my will to succeed. Today I commit to you the very best of me and promise that nothing and no one will ever have access to the space in my heart where you dwell."

Just about everyone in the room had tears in their eyes. This family that surrounded them knew the tremendous amount of stress and trauma these two had gone through and were proud that they had made it to this moment. It was even an added bonus that they hadn't succumbed to the pressure of needing the normal standard of wedding bells in order to solidify their union.

There would always be time for celebration and parties, but the reality was most people who may see you get married won't be around to pray with you for your marriage. These are the people that would do that for them. They knew if they needed anything it would be prayer, positive, loyal friends and family and they were completely satisfied with those that surrounded them in this moment.

After little J.J., Jack's rescued nephew, brought the rings to his grandfather to be blessed, Pastor Benett asked his wife, Mother Adele Benett, and Ivy's parents to join him as they stood around the two and prayed blessings over their union. Mother Benett prayed for strength, wisdom and courage that these two would continue to walk in faith and raise their children in faith and in the knowledge of God. Mother Kasey prayed for peace in their hearts and minds and a settling of the past so they could move forward without the painful residue of what was. Agent Kasey prayed for stability and wellness that they have both health and wealth to sustain them. Finally, Pastor Benett prayed for their continued safety and that any and every weapon that would form to come against this union would not work nor harm them or their children in Jesus' name, and they all said, "Amen."

"Now, by the power vested in me, I now pronounce you man and wife. Son, you may now salute your bride!"

Everyone in the room clapped their hands and cheered as Jack grabbed ahold of his new wife and kissed her passionately. When her lips met his the warmth of his mouth set a fire ablaze in Ivy's heart that rushed through her entire body. She wrapped her arms around his neck and continued the embrace as she realized they had made it! The sound of clapping hands from their family seemed to disappear in their ears as their minds went back to the very first time Jack kissed her.

They had been out quite a few times and although they enjoyed each other's company very much, Ivy wasn't sure if he was really interested romantically because Jack was so careful with his affection. He was always the gentleman as his father and mother had taught him to be, but Jack was a passionate man and the Navy disciplined him on when and where it was safe to exercise that passion. He knew if he kissed her, it would lead to him seeking the privilege to kiss her forever so, he waited.

Over time, Jack had proven to Ivy that everything he waited to do, was well worth the wait. So, as she thought about that night when he surprised her with a kiss in the parking lot of her favorite local gems, the NCG Theatre at Courtland Center, that same feeling of joy overwhelmed her now. They hugged each other tightly very satisfied in how they had chosen to begin their lives as man and wife.

Chapter 25

The family had all pitched in to make this evening beautiful. Jack and Ivy, if anything, were quite easy to please and didn't ask for much. For their reception meal their mothers prepared their mutual favorite – breakfast! The dining room table was set with a beautiful arrangement of fresh fruit and pastries that surrounded the hot chafers filled with crispy, Applewood smoked bacon, spicy maple sausage, hash browns sautéed with sweet onions and bell peppers, fluffy scrambled eggs and, Jack's favorite, buttermilk pancakes. The Benett's and the Kasey's all sat around the long oak dining room table for the first time as one big happy family.

"Ahem!" Jupiter explained while tapping the glass with his knife. "I would like to um… to make a toast here."

Everyone quieted their conversation and looked toward Jupiter to hear his speech.

Ivy sat smiling from ear to ear as her head rested gently on her husband's shoulder. One arm was wrapped under his and the other sat atop her tummy.

"This toast is not so much to my baby brother," Jupiter said, "but to my new baby sister, Ivy. A couple years ago Jackie went into a real tough shell when we thought we'd lost J.J. and, honestly, we weren't sure we would get him back. But we did. Even though he's always been a good man, he's become an even better man with you. It's because of you that we have our brother back and any love that strong I know has to be from God," Jupiter said, sincerely.

He motioned for his brothers to stand up with him. Jasper, Jason and Jordyn Sr., all stood tall with their glasses in hand lifting them into the air.

"To Ivy!"

They all clinked glasses together and drank to the love that gave them back a piece of their heart. Ivy was again buried in her handkerchief trying to stop the tears from flowing. She no idea her new brothers thought so much of her. She hadn't had an opportunity to spend as much time with them as she would have liked, but it was such a relief to know that they were able to feel, and see, how much she adored their brother and would do him no harm.

Both families were pleased to see that the other would be in good hands. It was wonderful for Ivy's brother to see that she would be well looked after even though he lived so far away. James Jr. had been unsure about whether or not this union would good for his baby sister, but being here and able to witness this all for himself was a blessing. He wouldn't have too much to say this evening, he would leave the toast to their eldest sibling, Ivonne.

"I'm kind of speechless because what Jupiter said about my sister is much of what I had planned to say about his brother," Ivonne laughed. "I guess if we needed anymore confirmation that these two people belong together, now we have it. The truth is that although my sister has always been a very driven and purpose-filled individual, she has had a very hard time with limits and boundaries," Ivonne jokingly said clearing her throat. "We all knew what she was capable of, but we worried about her because she gives so much and loves so hard and… and she will push the limits just to prove she's strong enough to handle even the most painful of losses. We didn't know how or when the Lord would put the pieces of her heart back together and then He sent us you, Jackson. Just as Jupiter stated that she brought you back to them, you have brought her back to us, in more ways than one," Ivonne said trying to hold back the tears.

With his arm around Ivy's shoulder, Jack pulled her close and sweetly kissed the side of her face. She closed her eyes and smiled with joy.

Ivonne lifted her glass and her siblings stood with her. "This toast is to you, Jackson."

Once again they all clinked glasses. Ivy looked around and she was so elated to see that her wedding day had turned out better than she could ever imagine. It was 11:58 p.m. when Jack stood up next to his lovely wife to have words.

"It's almost midnight and before we depart I would love the honor of dancing with my wife," As he held his hand out to grab hers, he continued, "Mrs. Benett, may I have this dance?" Ivy placed her hand in his and he helped her out of her seat.

The family watched them walk into the living room where the furniture had been pushed to the outer walls. The purple lights bounced against the dim candles barely burning as Jack and Ivy danced together for the first time as man and wife. They danced slowly to the tune of *'Candy'* by Big Mabelle, a song that soulfully expressed such accurate sentiment of how Ivy felt about her new husband. It was her favorite song from one of her favorite blues singers that just happen to have gotten her recording start in her Great-Aunt Christine's orchestra back in 1944. Now it was the song that would always bring recollection of this day when she married the man of her dreams. They danced through midnight and then, finally said their goodnight's to their family and headed home.

While Ivy was out with her sisters that day preparing for the wedding, Jack and his brothers had spent half the day cleaning up their house. It no longer looked like bachelor pad, but a home that's just perfect for him and his growing family. Although there was still painting and detail to add to the nursery, every room had been straightened up neatly and Ivy was so surprised to see what he had done.

He held her hand as he walked her through the halls of their home where he had gotten dozens of red roses to be placed on every surface. When he got her to the bedroom she was even more amazed. It was nothing at all like the night before with Jack's work and clothes on everything.

Kayla's wedding gift was to turn Jack and Ivy's simple bedroom into a romantic boudoir starting with a complete makeover of their honey walnut finished king sleigh bed. She replaced the simple jersey cotton linen Jack had on the bed with all black 1500 thread count satin weave linen complete with a grey down feather comforter. Black and silver pillows were stacked against the leather padded headboard. The flickering light of flameless candles everywhere gave the room a soft romantic glow as the scent of the fresh roses and Victoria Secret's Love Spell enveloped the room.

The family had offered to treat the newlyweds to a weekend at a hotel of their choosing, but the couple wanted to be at home. They would have the house to themselves with Melanie at her grandparents for the weekend and with all that had occurred over the last few months they had plenty of making up to do. Although they were both tired from the day they weren't at all too tired to consummate their marriage. Ironically, this couple, who were not strangers to physical intimacy and had been missing it anxiously for the last nine months, was in no rush to get home and jump into bed. Of course, they were excited about this night, but more excited about forever.

Ivy was in a very different physical state than she was the last time they had made love. It was an amazing night and also the night in which she had conceived and since then so much about her body had changed. She never had a problem in the bedroom, but she was very anxious about how to do what she used to do with two babies protruding from her stomach. For the first time in their relationship Ivy was nervous about whether or not she could please Jack and on her wedding night, she did not want to leave her husband unsatisfied.

Jack, unaware of her apprehension, like most men cared nothing about how many babies were curled up inside her, he was just proud that he had put them there and it made him want her even more. Although he had been concerned with how well her body had healed from the accident, she was much stronger now than when they were supposed to be married so he wasn't at all hesitant. He missed having her and although he was ready for her he was in no rush. After almost two years of holding back, Jack could finally give her everything and had every intention of taking his time and taking care of his wife.

Jack walked over to the nightstand and pushed play on the CD player and *'Hey Now'*, by Carl Thomas, began to play softly. He looked intently at his new wife and began to unravel that handsome paisley tie from around his neck and undo the top buttons of the off white dress shirt that graced his massive chest. After removing the silver monogram cufflinks, Jack removed all the other jewelry and set it on the dresser. Everything, except his wedding ring.

Ivy, reading his movements, reached up and began to take out the flowers and pins that were holding up the bun in her hair. Once the last purple rose was taken from her ponytail, Ivy's brown hair began to fall onto her shoulders and surround her face. She grinned just barely showing her dimples as she looked across the room at her husband walking back towards her. Ivy turned her back to him and looked at him anxiously over her shoulder.

"Babe… I know this is silly…" she began as Jack stood behind her and began to rub her neck and shoulders. "I'm a little nervous," she confessed

"Why are you nervous?" he laughed.

"I've never done this… pregnant… my body is a lot different than it was the last time and…"

"Sugar," he interrupted as he began to kiss her neck and slowly unzip her dress revealing the matching black lace camisole and panty that adorned her body. "You don't have to do anything," he said gently pulling her arms out of their sleeves. "I got this…." he whispered in her ear seductively and she shivered as her dress fell to the floor.

Jack helped his near naked wife onto their bed so she could be comfortable as he removed the rest of the garments that covered her. He stared at her. He thought briefly about all the hesitations and doubts he may have ever had about how ready or not he was about making a lifetime commitment, but being with her at that moment reminded him how immature he had been.

Ivy closed her eyes and took a deep breath as he began to kiss every part of her body that he knew she was sensitive to. From the space on her neck, between her ear and collarbone, to the inside of her thighs, Jack caressed her with his lips until she was holding tight to the bedframe behind her. It wasn't long before Ivy was begging him to give her everything. He slid up to her face and began to kiss her madly and as she ripped open his shirt. Not aware of her own strength, his buttons flew off to multiple parts of the room. Her hands moved swiftly to his belt as she wanted to undress him from head to toe, but he wouldn't let her.

Jack, slowly kissing the bottom of her ears, and whispered, "I told you... I got this."

With one hand, he moved her hands behind her head and, with the other, he searched between her thighs for the fingerprints he had left the last time. Her body responded to the familiar warmth of his hand and she moaned in delight as he literally pushed all of her buttons. As he turned her into a river, he continued to kiss her neck until he had managed to move her onto her on her side and position himself behind her.

When he finally entered her, Jack had one hand full of her breast and with the other he maneuvered her body into a position she'd never been in ...but would never forget. He melted into her like the delicate blending of rough shards of dark chocolate into thick, hot, heavy cream – a combination that created nothing less than magic in both touch and taste. Every kiss, every touch, every stroke was wrapped in intense passion on a level of intimacy neither of them had ever anticipated. He breathed heavily on her shoulder as the sweat that ran from his neck to the center of his chest was like oil that keep their bodies moving smoothly against one another with ease.

Ivy never wanted anything or anybody more. As much as she wanted to respond more physically then she could at this moment, Jack's guidance ensured that neither of them went lacking. Sounds of pleasure filled the room as their bodies collapsed in total and complete satisfaction.

Finally for the first time there was no guilt attached to their desire. This was her husband. She was his wife and with honored commitment, they could have each other as passionately as they always wanted.

Just as he promised, Jack took care of her in every way until she was fast asleep and nestled comfortably in his arms. He stayed awake and watched her sleep, just waiting for her to start humming. Once the humming began he knew she would sleep through the night without any terrors and then he could go to sleep in peace.

Chapter 26

It was Tuesday morning and Jack was going back to work. Melanie was home, and he and Ivy's life together as a family had officially begun. After their weekend of passion had come to a close, Jack promised Ivy that they would have an official honeymoon and he would take her wherever she wanted to go. She was so easy to please, he knew she wouldn't ask for much and as long as they were together she would be satisfied. Once the babies made their arrival, they would have a full house and she would soon want that trip.

They still had a few more weeks before the due date so they planned to focus on finishing new nursery and concentrate on completing their therapy. The next session with Dr. Gilbert was this afternoon after their appointment with the OB/GYN so Jack was only going to work a half day. He wouldn't dare miss another appointment.

After being awaken to the smell of bacon, Jack began to prepare himself to go back to work while his loving wife was preparing Melanie for daycare. Ivy was in the kitchen giving Melanie her breakfast and putting

Jack's breakfast on a clean white china plate. Her hair was in a messy ponytail wrapped in her black silk scarf and she was dressed in a very comfortable blue tube dress when Jack walked into the kitchen behind her. He grabbed a palm full of her backside and leaned down to kiss her on her shoulder.

"Oh!" she exclaimed.

"Good morning, my wife," he said happily, with his chin nestled in her neck.

"Good morning, my husband," she said as she turned around and kissed him back full on the mouth. "Are you ready for your breakfast?" she asked biting her bottom lip.

"Hmmm…. I do have a little time," he moaned as he started to tickle her by lightly biting into her neck.

Ivy laughed and tried lean her head over to stop the tickling.

"I meant food babe. Real food," she laughed. Melanie thought it was funny as well.

"Daddy you tickled Movy!" she laughed with fruit loops on the side of her face.

Jack went over to his daughters chair and started tickling her and she screamed in delight. He took a seat next to her and Ivy brought him his plate of bacon, eggs and hash browns, with fresh grapes and strawberries and a tall glass of cold cranberry juice.

"The doctor's appointment is at what time again?" he asked as he began to eat.

"The first with the OB/GYN is at one and then we see Dr. Gilbert at three."

"Right, right... okay."

"But you have that meeting with my dad at the Rhema Café at two. Kayla is going to bring me downtown and I'll meet you at Dr. Gilbert's office at three."

"Okay sounds like a plan."

"Melanie is all set to go to daycare and Mommy will pick her up for us at 2:30 and we'll pick her up on our way home."

Jack never had his days so clear for him before he met her. Ivy brought balance and organization to his busy life and he was proud that she belonged to him. He had longed for being able to start his mornings with her this way and now that he could, it seemed too good to be true. With plenty to be thankful for, he gratefully packed up his things and his daughter, kissed his wife and headed out the door for work.

It didn't take long for Ivy's day to get started and begin flying by fast. No sooner than Jack was out the door, she was setting up her computer in the living room. Before she sat down and got comfortable, she loaded the washing machine, the dishwasher, took a shower and dressed for the day. By the time she had settled in front of the computer it was 11:52 a.m. and she didn't have too much time before Jack would be back to pick her up.

Ivy opened her Word file where she had started to write her book that was so appropriately entitled, *The Edge of Water*. When she first got home from the hospital all she knew was that she wanted to record her experience with Jack to create this literary work of art in the hopes that many other Christian ladies with her background would be able to identify with. With the intent to fictionalize with the changing of dates, times, names and other minor details, her reality was turning into a very entertaining novel.

Ivy found herself so involved in the writing that it would cause her own excitement to peak from not knowing from day-to-day where the story would actually go. Although it began as her own experience that she wanted to share, she found the story leaning its way more toward Jack as the lead character versus herself. At first she was a little jealous of the main male character of whom she had based on Jack because he had somehow become the dominant figure in her story. So she found herself again at Humble Road and, like any true artist, regardless of what she intended, in order to release what God had placed inside, Ivy submitted to the direction of the story. Once she did that, the jealously began to fade as she realized the honor it was to be able to write more than just her story, but their story. She continued to write until Jack picked her up for their doctor's appointment.

She had showed him all the sonograms and pictures and let him hear all the heartbeat recordings she had made, but this would be their first time seeing their babies together. Jack was very excited when the doctor came into the room to start the picture show as they would be taking 3D pictures of the babies and he couldn't wait to see them. Although they had both agreed to wait until delivery to find out the sexes of the babies they were becoming impatient and this appointment just may be the breaking point for them both.

The doctor was congratulating them on their marriage when he started taking pictures and Jack began fighting his hardest to hold back the tears, but Ivy didn't bother fighting. She cried tears of joy as they saw their beautiful babies smiling and holding hands inside the womb. They relished the moment and were talking all about how cute the babies were while Dr. Cooper got Ivy cleaned up and ready to prep them for the birth. Ivy had been cleared for a vaginal birth as long as her blood pressure stayed normal and the babies were in a safe position. Just in case, the doctor had walked them through the Cesarean process and reminded them of all the instructions he had given them.

"Okay, mom and dad, I think we're all set and ready to have some babies! Are we sure we don't want to know their sex?" Dr. Cooper asked. "This is your last time to find out because after today I won't need to see you until you're ready for the birth."

Jack and Ivy looked at each other both unsure of what they wanted. They laughed.

"I want to know," Jack finally admitted. "I mean the baby shower is coming up and we should let people know right?"

"The people? What about us?" Ivy laughed. "We need to know so we can finish the nursery and… I just don't want to wait anymore," she confessed. Ivy was ready.

"You sure?" Jack asked, for the last time.

"I'm sure," Ivy confirmed, smiling.

"Okay Dr. C, tell us what we're having." Jack said as he squeezed Ivy's hand.

She took a deep breath and closed her eyes tight as she waited to hear the news. Dr. Cooper turned his chair around and grabbed their file.

"Alright then, Mr. and Mrs. Benett you are the proud parents of identical baby…um let me see here," he said teasing them looking up and down his files.

"Really! Are you serious Dr. C?" Ivy exclaimed jokingly.

"Okay… okay", he laughed, "I'm done teasing you. Congratulations, you're having two little boys!"

"YES!" Jack and Ivy shouted in unison as they high fived each other than hugged tightly. This was very exciting news as they got exactly what they prayed for. Two handsome boys, of which, Ivy already had the perfect names for she just hoped and prayed Jack would agree with her idea, but that could wait. Now it was time to get to their next appointment of which they were much less apprehensive about than the last time. They had great news to share with Dr. Gilbert.

They walked out of the doctor's office together feeling very satisfied. Kayla was right out front waiting to pick up Ivy and Jack was leaving her to meet with her dad. He kissed his wife and assured her he would be on time for their appointment.

"I'll see you in a few, Sugar," he confirmed, once again with his hand firmly on her waist.

"Okay, babe."

Ivy kissed him back sweetly on his cheek and he returned by catching her lips. They were nearly engulfed in their embraced when interrupted by Kayla honking her horn. With her window open, she cleared her throat loudly.

"Hey, hey!" she yelled. "Maybe just say goodbye and not give the people a show out here!" she joked.

"Yeah, whatever," Jack laughed as he let go of his wife and helped her into the car. "You just make sure you take care of my wife you understand?"

"You just make sure you're on time, my brother." Kayla shot back.

"That's where we're at Kayla?" Jack laughed closing the door. "Thought we were better than that, but it's cool."

"Okay see you later babe. I love you," Ivy said interrupting Jack and Kayla's playful exchange.

"I love you, too," Jack responded.

Ivy, smiling with her eyes, leaned her head to the side and just quietly watched him walk to his truck as they drove off. She had gotten in this odd habit of just watching him with wonder and giving thanks to God for blessing her so greatly with this man. Not the one she thought she always wanted, but with the one she never knew she needed. When Jack first proposed he stated that she was proof of God's love for her and it was her exact same feeling in that moment.

"Girl, you all the way gone," Kayla laughed out loud pulling Ivy out of her thoughts.

"What do you mean?"

"You just a daydreaming over there."

"Oh, well you know, what can I say?" Ivy laughed. "I'm happy."

"As well you should be. I'm happy for you, but I'm also gonna laugh at you a little bit."

"I know you are."

"So did you two finally cave in and find out what the sex of the babies are?"

"Yes, we did, and would you believe we're having identical twin boys?"

"Actually, yes, I can believe it. I saw the chart three months ago and I've been buying the most adorable things and hiding them from you," Kayla confessed finally relieved of this secret.

Ivy laughed. "I can't believe you. You knew this whole time?"

"Yup! And so did your mom because I told her. Your baby shower is next week. We had to know."

"Yeah, okay,"

Ivy was on this serious pretzel kick and when she wanted one there was no stopping her. So Kayla went to the Valley to Auntie Annie's to get some pretzels sticks, made fresh with no salt, and spicy nacho cheese to satisfy her cousins pregnant appetite.

As they pulled up to the Dryden building downtown where Dr. Gilbert's office was, Ivy was licking her fingers in delight. She climbed out of the car with her purse and the rest of her pretzels, thanked Kayla for the ride and as quick as she could, wobbled inside to make her appointment on time.

Chapter 27

Ivy, glowing of hormones and happiness made her way up to the 21st floor yet again to see Dr. Gilbert for her second joint session with her man, and her first with her husband. As she wobbled back in to the office she was couldn't wait to share with Julia the good news. It was odd, but she felt like her therapist would be proud. That really meant something to her to be able to share with Dr. Gilbert that her time invested into ensuring that she and Jack would have a successful relationship, was not in vain.

It had taken them weeks of therapy to get here. Conversations that forced them to take a very honest look into the decisions they had made and how they had contributed much to their own sabotage and it had not been easy. The only easy part was building up a case against each other, finding fault and pointing out all of the difficult personality traits that aren't as easy to love around, but Ivy was feeling so grown up in that she had accepted the truth about what it really meant to love another person. That understanding had gotten her to the altar with the man she loved, with no crowds, no fanfare, no stunning white gown or sparkling veil and happier than she ever thought she could be.

"Well, good afternoon, Ivy. I'm guessing you had a pretty good weekend! Once again you are just glowing!"

"Thank you, Julia," Ivy said blushing.

"Am I detecting a little bit more than hormones here? What's up with you dear?"

"Julia, I think I've just had the best weekend of my life! So far that is."

"Oh really? Well come sit down here and tell me what you did."

Julia walked Ivy over to the big leather chairs that sat on either side of the matching leather sofa and helped her to get comfortable. Ivy liked the comfort of the couch very much, but it was proving more difficult to get up from it so she took to the chair and Dr. Gilbert brought over the matching ottoman for her to rest her feet on. Once she was nice and comfy and settled she began to share.

"Well, for one, Jack and I took your advice and we got married Friday evening."

Julia's eyes lit up with pride as if it was the news of her own children tying the knot. She had seen many people, but there was something so special about these two that, unbeknownst to them, she kept them lifted in prayer. Although she prays for all that come into her office, Dr. Gilbert knew when it came to Jack and Ivy, she was on special assignment from God to see them through to the next level. In this moment she felt like she had indeed started on the right path and attending well to her assignment.

"That is so awesome! I'm…I'm just …" she was really finding it hard to get her words together and Julia Gilbert is never speechless. She cleared her throat and took a deep breath. "Okay, tell me how it all happened."

"It was absolutely beautiful! Only our immediate families were present and his dad, who is a pastor, married us in his home. It was just…" Ivy paused with tears in her eyes, "It was really just perfect. I couldn't have asked for a better way to get married."

Julia handed her a few tissues from the desk and kept a couple for herself as she, too, had tears welling up in her eyes. Ivy shared with her how last

Thursday evening had gone from their date after therapy, to the night terror that Jack witnessed and how she was convinced in that moment that there was nothing to wait for. Tears of joy continued to drip lightly form her eyes as she talked about how wonderful it had been to have their families' support and how the surprise of her father's presence was the icing on the cake.

"Sounds like it was just perfect."

"I mean, I can't complain at all. It was perfect and it keeps getting better."

"Oh yeah? How do you mean?"

"We just left the doctor and finally found out the sex of our babies. It turns out we're getting just what we prayed for – two identical twin boys."

"Wow, well my goodness you have had an amazing couple of days! And thank the good Lord because you deserve it dear, you really do."

"Thank you, Dr. Gilbert, for everything. I really mean it. I know you went above and beyond for us and I thank God for you," Ivy said sincerely. She attempted to continue, but was interrupted by her phone that started to ring from her purse. "Excuse me

Julia, it's my father," she said, quickly as she picked up the phone. "Hello?"

"Ivy?"

"Hi Daddy."

"Hey, how you doing?"

"I'm great, how are you?"

"Doing okay. So you guys run late at the doctors today?"

"No sir, not late we anticipated being through about 1:45 so that wasn't bad. Why'd you think we were late?"

"Because Jack missed our appointment so I figured he was still with you."

"No, I haven't seen him since we left the doctors about an hour ago when he went to meet you. What do you mean he missed your appointment?" Ivy asked as the news sent a chill down her spine.

She wasn't about to let any fear get the best of her, everything was fine and she knew there had to be some explanation. Jack was just terrible at time management, more often than not, and it wasn't quite 3 p.m. so he wasn't late for their appointment yet. She stood up and walked over to the window as she rubbed her tummy to calm her nerves.

"I'm saying I've been here at the café since two and he hasn't shown up, so I thought you guys may have ran over at the doctor."

"Well, did you call him?"

"I did and it was going straight to voicemail."

"Okay, well, let me try to call him. He may have gotten stuck in traffic trying to get downtown."

"Okay, sounds good, call me and let me know. If you reach him tell him we can meet tomorrow."

"Will do. Thanks, Daddy."

Ivy hung up the phone and started dialing Jack without looking up at Julia. She didn't want her to see any fear on her face, not after all her confession of no longer letting the small things matter. She wasn't about to show one tiny bit of panic. Ivy would trust that all was well.

"Everything okay?" Dr. Gilbert asked. She wasn't ignorant to Ivy's change in tone and she knew something was a little off.

"Oh, yeah, everything's fine. Jack and my dad were supposed to meet at two before he came here, but apparently he got stuck in traffic or something because he didn't show up," Ivy said, finally looking up and laughing nervously. The phone started to ring and she was relieved. "Knowing Jack he found somebody in trouble and rushed to the rescue," she waited as the phone rang until it went to voicemail but didn't bother to leave a message.

"It went to voicemail?"

"Yeah. He'll call me right back when he sees I've called."

"Okay, well, until he calls back let's get you back over here to a seat and you can tell me more about the wedding." Dr. Gilbert suggested, moving over to her desk chair.

Ivy stood still at the corner of the desk with her phone held tight in her hand waiting for it to ring. She knew everything was okay, but her body wasn't going to relax until she was sure everything was truly okay. Her idea was to keep calm as not to alarm Julia, but it wasn't coming off very well at all. Julia could tell she was nervous and decided to stand next Ivy so that she felt supported even if her feelings of fear were irrational. They were both relieved when Ivy's phone started to ring and she began to smile. It was Jack. She looked at the phone, dimples deep in anticipation of hearing his voice before she answered.

"Hey babe, where are you? Daddy said…" Ivy paused mid-sentence. "Hello?"

The color of Ivy's face seem to turn pale instantaneously causing great distress to every single one of Julia's senses. She was an agent in the bureau for twenty years before she settled into therapy and she knew what that look meant.

"Ivy… Ivy?" Dr. Gilbert called her name as she saw Ivy had frozen solid. Her eyes were wide, and her phone began to slowly slide out of her trembling hand and down the side of her face. Julia grabbed Ivy's hand and started to shake her lightly hoping to get her attention. "Ivy! What did Jack say? What's wrong?"

With water welling up in her eyes like shields of glass, in a low raspy and airy voice she answered Julia.

"It wasn't Jack…" Ivy said, hardly believing her own words. As one, lonely tear fell slowly down her rosy, brown cheek, she turned and looked Dr. Gilbert in her eyes and said, "It was Lisa."

The Edge of Light
The Final Installment of the "Edge" Series

About The Author

Nina David Lewis is a proud native of Flint, Michigan, where her love for the creative and performance art was birthed and cultivated. She developed into a colorful writer and has written, directed and produced numerous stage plays. Along with performance art and leadership curriculums, her work has been utilized across the country.

The beloved *Purple Rose* of L.A., Lady Nina, is the comedic host of the *Life with Nina* radio show that airs live every Friday night. She is most proud of her work as the First Lady of the Esther Lady Society International, in which she works with girls to teach them the value of being a lady in today's society.

Nina is a Dream Therapist and Life Coach with goals of helping people find their purpose in life.

For booking:
www.ndlewis.com
info@ndlewis.com

Social Media
IG: @LifeWithNinaD
FB: Facebook.com/LifeWithNina